Upcoming Titles

of

True Stories

1. Baby Robbers
2. They Say She Broke The Rule
3. Bradley vs. The State of Michigan
4. Sexy Red

Fiction Titles

5. Child of Exile
6. Time of Death
7. Twisted Society

And more

Chocolate Mama

By
Helen Bradley Hall

CHOCOLATE MAMA
A
Helen Bradley Hall
Copyright © 2011

ISBN 978-0-9658140-9-6

LCCN 2011905137

Editor: Ray Glandon

Bradley's publishing Co.

About the Author

Helen Bradley Hall was born August 24, 1973.With her high school diploma in hand, she enrolled at The National Institute of Technology, now known as Everest Institute. In May 2006, Helen graduated from NIT with a grade point average of 97.6, receiving her Medical Assistant certificate. While attending school, Helen had written her second book, titled, *The Battle Within.*

Helen obtained a job working in a doctor's office as a medical assistant and was later diagnosed with Lupus in 2006, but she continued to work in the medical field. In 2007, Helen ended her career in the medical field but continued her career as an author. She currently attends AIU online, seeking to obtain her associates and bachelors degree in criminal justice, with plans of eventually obtaining a law degree. This is her third book, and she is working on many others. Helen continues to stay in the Lord, giving him the glory and honor for all that she has done, and acknowledges that she is nothing without the Lord Jesus.

Special thanks

First, I'd like to give thanks to my Lord Jesus Christ. He has sustained me through all my illnesses in helping me to pursue all my dreams. I'd like to thank my children, husband, and mother for being so supportive. I also want to thank my editor, Ray Glandon, for doing such a wonderful job. Last, but not least, I'd like to thank everyone who purchased my book, making my success possible!

Preface

Life can be filled with such disappointments, it can be too much to bear at times. We all have experienced life tragedies, some worse than others.
In this novel, sadly, you will see how sometimes even family can be your worst enemy. But the dilemma is, what do you do? Are you to accept such things, or should you do something about it? I can tell you this, losing loved ones can be a hard pill to swallow, and when your family is the cause of tragedies that can be difficult as well. In this novel you will experience loss. So, I recommend that you sit back and enjoy *Chocolate Mama* and let your mind wander with the story. You will be captivated by the action involved in this novel. I hope this will open your mind to the possibility that anything can happen.

Table of Contents

Chapter One

The prom

Liza Dozier, excited about this being her senior year, was due to graduate in six months. She was very pretty and was voted the prettiest girl at her school. Liza was five-three, one hundred and fifteen pounds. She had long, wavy black hair and beautiful chocolate skin. Her chocolate brown eyes blended with her skin complexion. She was popular, so all the boys wanted to be her boyfriend. She was already spoken for, as she had been dating the captain of their school football team for four years now.

Berlin Hamgorium was voted the most handsome boy in school. He was drop-dead gorgeous. Liza and Berlin were the perfect couple. Berlin had an olive complexion, and long, dark red wavy hair. His eyes were a chestnut brown color, and his body was like a time bomb, explosive. He was six-one and, one hundred and ninety pounds of solid muscle. They dreamed of a successful life together running their very own clothing line. Berlin came from a rich family, and so did Liza, but nothing like Berlin's family. Berlin and Liza were graduating in six months. They both planned on going to Ivy League colleges for fashion designing. Liza's best friend, Connie Marled, chose to go to a local college. They all had been friends since kindergarten.

Throughout school, Liza fought a lot with girls that were jealous of her. Although she was smart and beautiful, Liza packed a mean punch; she was a little scrapper. Liza was the oldest of seven children; she had two sisters and four brothers. They were each a year apart. Liza appeared to be happy, but deep down inside she wasn't. She hid a secret so deep, she was truly a mess mentally. She talked to no one in her home, not even her own parents. She felt free in school, where she would smile and talk. Berlin had a secret he was hiding as well. He never showed any emotions, so no one knew what was going on in his life. Liza and Berlin were going shopping for the prom. Liza's cell phone rang. She looked at her phone to see who was calling. It was her mom. "Yes, Mom."

"Hello to you, Liza. I was calling to tell you that since it's your prom, instead of a spending limit of three thousand, how about four thousand?" All she could hear was Liza yelling in excitement, "Thanks Mom, you're the best, I love you so much." Before Estrada could say it back, Liza hung up.

Berlin knew why she was so happy; all he could do was smile. Either way, the prom was covered. Berlin, clearing his throat, spoke, "My dad is giving us his limo for the night." Connie and Liza grabbed their chest.

"You mean that pretty Hummer Limo?"

"Yup, that's it."

"This is going to be the best prom ever," Liza said.

They left the building, heading towards Berlin's 2008 Mercedes truck, and Berlin and Liza decided that instead of going to the mall to buy the dress and tux, they would make their own. They went to the biggest and most expensive fabric store in town. They were both talented in that area, so why not? Last year Liza made uniforms for the cheerleading squad, and they were the most unique and beautiful attire you would find. That same year Berlin made the seniors caps and gowns.

Liza had already decided to use one hundred percent silk to make her prom dress, but it was going to look more like a gown fit for a queen. Their colors were sapphire blue and a light cream. Liza and Berlin both agreed that those colors would be perfect. Connie and her prom date were wearing peach and silver. Liza and Berlin shopped as fast as they could for their material so they could go back to his house and begin to design their prom attire. They went to work in his sewing room right away. They were two weeks away from their prom, and they were excited. Berlin had something else planned that night for the prom.

On the day of the prom, Liza hadn't seen or heard from him all day. She began to worry. She called his cell phone, no answer. She knew he would be there to pick her up at 7:30 p.m. because the prom started at nine. It was 2:00 p.m., and Liza felt uneasy. She should have heard from him by now. Blowing off the fact that he never answered his phone, she ran upstairs to run a bubble bath. She only had a couple of hours before her hair appointment. Grabbing her clothes out of the closet, she threw them onto the bed quickly while undressing for her bubble bath. Entering the bathroom, the steam from the hot tub of water left a fog over the room; she inhaled the hot misty air. As she entered the water, she let out a sigh of relief. A knock at the door broke her relaxation. She yelled, "What! Can't I relax for a change?" All she heard was her sister, Sage yelling, "Hurry up in there already. I want to shower, too, and all the other bathrooms are taken."

"Wait your turn," Liza shot back snobbishly. "I'll be out in a minute." Twenty minutes later, Liza came trotting out of the bathroom with a smirk on her face. She knew Sage was angry that she took so long. Sage, rolling her eyes, spoke, "You are so mean, Liza." Liza ignored her, walked in her room, and laid out her prom dress. She was going to the mall today to find shoes to match her dress, along with matching accessories. Keanu, Liza's sister, whizzed past their mom, running to Liza's room with the gift she had bought Liza for her prom. With a smile on her face, she said, "Open it!"
Liza asked, "What is this?"
"Just open it; it's something I bought for you today." Liza tore the paper off the box quickly. When she opened the box, tears came to her eyes. She was speechless. All she could say was, "Keanu." After she

got herself together, she was able to speak. "Keanu, these are beautiful, these are better than the ones I saw at the mall. These match my prom gown perfectly, and they are going to match my shoes, too." She grabbed Keanu, giving her a big hug, thanking her for the earrings. Keanu left with a smile saying, "I knew you would like them, Liza."

Looking at her watch, she noticed the time; she had to get to her hair appointment. It was 3:15 p.m. She grabbed her purse and flew down the stairs. Liza kissed Keanu on the cheek, thanking her once again for the earrings and exited the door like a tornado. Before she could pull off, her cell phone rang. It was Berlin. She answered dryly, "Hello."

He began to talk fast. "Let me explain before you bite my head off."

She interrupted him asking, "Just where have you been all day, Berlin? I have been worried sick ... "

"Baby, I'm fine, I had some business to attend to before the prom."

"Is everything all right?"

"Yeah, everything is good, but enough about me. How was your day?"

"Great, now that I have heard from you."

"That's good, but are you busy now, Liza?"

"As a matter of fact, I'm on my way to the hair salon. I'll be there awhile because I'm getting a manicure and a pedicure."

"All right, I guess I'll see you at seven."

"Ok, I love you, B."

"I love you too, Liza."

Talking on the phone made the drive seem short. Pulling in the parking lot, she spotted Connie's car. She was waiting inside the salon for her. They planned on getting ready for the prom together. They had their pedicures done first, so their feet would be dry before they left. Their hair was the last thing to be done. At first they were undecided on what style to get, but they made up their minds. Once they were done, Liza looked like a movie star. Admiring herself in the mirror, she finally stopped long enough to pay the beautician. Leaving, both of them felt like they were models out of a magazine. They hopped in their cars and headed to Liza's house. They eagerly walked inside ready to get dressed for the prom. It was now six o'clock. They had an hour to get dressed. Connie, with her prom dress in hand, ran up the stairs. When she saw Liza's prom gown, she fell in love with it and was speechless. She had never seen a prom gown like it. All Connie could say was, "Liza this is beautiful. This is a gown made for a queen. You do realize all the girls are going to hate you?"

"Who cares, Connie? They can hate all they want." She laughed while heading for the bathroom to get dressed. She remembered that she forgot to pick up her shoes. She yelled, "Mom, Mom!" Estrada quickly entered the bathroom asking, "What is it child?"

"Mom, I forgot my shoes for the prom."
Estrada laughed so hard tears came to her eyes. Liza had no time to get them, and the gown wouldn't be right without those shoes.

Estrada spoke, "I called the salon at 5:30 to see if you were still there, and you were. So I had Sage run up and get the shoes you were talking about all week." Sage had the shoes and necklace in Liza's room already. Liza opened the box and they were the exact same shoes she wanted. She gave Sage a hug that was big enough for the world. Liza ran back to the bathroom to finish getting dressed. She stood in the mirror once she was done. She couldn't believe how beautiful the gown was. It was elegant, which was the look she wanted. Leaving the restroom, she noticed Connie was just as beautiful in her dress. They each put on a robe so they could do their makeup. They were finally ready to go downstairs. They knew they were knockouts and that everyone was at the bottom of the staircase waiting for them to come down. Before they left the room, they held hands and wished each other good luck and a great future.

Everyone's mouth dropped as soon as they hit the top staircase. Estrada was in awe of Liza's beauty. She began to snap pictures of the two while they walked down the stairs. Estrada began to cry because her first baby girl, Liza, was soon becoming a woman. She was already a young lady. Estrada spoke, "You girls look stunning." The doorbell rang. It was Berlin and Dexter. Liza didn't want to be seen yet, so she and Connie went into the other room. The two young men greeted everyone and walked to the family room to wait. Connie and Liza entered the room. Berlin and Dexter were speechless. Gazing at the two, they finally spoke in unison, "You ladies look beautiful." Blushing, Liza and Connie said, "Thank you." They headed toward the foyer to take pictures before they left for the prom. Smiling at how good they all looked, Estrada said, "Have a safe night." The girl's were on cloud nine. Before they were seated in the limo, the guys gave the ladies their corsages, and they posed for a picture outside the limo. The girl's spoke, "You guys look so handsome." Just before Liza got into the limo, Estrada kissed her on the cheek and whispered, "Remember the curfew, and have a good time."

The chauffeur was dressed in black and white and was very polite. His passengers were cuddled up with each other all the way to the prom. When they pulled up, everybody knew who it was, Berlin and Liza with their two best friends. Liza and Berlin were the two richest kids in the school. Everyone knew their entire families. Everyone ate at the Dozier's restaurant, and everybody knew who the Hamgorium's were. Heck, every kid in the school wore Hamgorium designer jeans. As soon as they stepped out, a couple of jealous schoolmates turned their noses up at them. Liza and Berlin didn't care; they walked right into the prom and began their night. For Liza, this night was like a fairy tale; she was the princess and Berlin was her prince.

The night was perfect. They danced the night away. Laughing and having a great time, they decided to grab a table and have a seat for a while. It was almost time to announce the prom king and queen of the year. The girl that was announcing the king and queen this year was so excited, she just tore open the envelope. She said, "Excuse me, may I have your attention? This year's prom king and queen are, Berlin

Hamgorium and Liza Dozier." Not totally surprised by it, they walked arm- in- arm up on the stage. Liza was given a tiara, a bouquet of flowers, and a wand. Berlin was given a crown, robe, and a staff. The crowd chanted, "Speech, speech." Berlin bowed, saying, "You first, my dear." Liza, clearing her throat, spoke. "This has truly been a great senior year. I'll miss you all. I wish everyone here the best. Thank you." They all cheered for Liza because they knew she was going to make it. Berlin stepped to the microphone. "I know I may have been a S.O.B. to some of you here, but I'm glad to have come across such good people. I've grown from it, and I thank you." The crowd cheered for him as well because they knew he would make it, too. Each of them had promising futures, and the colleges they were to attend were topnotch.

Once the crowd died down, he spoke again. "There's something else I need to say." Turning toward Liza, he grabbed her hand and stared into her eyes. He spoke softly, saying, "Liza, we have been in love for four years now, and we have known each other since preschool. That is proof that we are meant to be together." He paused before he began to finish his statement. "When you called me earlier, I told you I had some business to take care of. That business was you, Liza." He reached into his pocket. Liza couldn't move. Berlin bent down on one knee, and the crowd let out a loud cheer. They silenced themselves to see what he was going to do. Once he was down, he opened the box. Liza's eyes were the size of silver dollars, looking at the ring. He continued to speak. "Liza D. Dozier, will you marry me?" She was speechless, but this was what she wanted, too. She said. "Yes! Berlin, yes, I will marry you." They hugged and kissed while the crowd went absolutely wild. They walked off the stage, holding hands. Dexter and Connie hugged them both and congratulated them on their engagement, as did everyone else.

They had the dance floor to themselves for the prom king and queen dance. The ring he put on her finger was a rock. Liza had never seen a diamond so big. Once the song was over, Liza ran outside to the limo to call her mother from the car phone. When she answered and heard Liza's voice, she thought Liza was in trouble because she was crying. She wasted no time asking, "Liza what is wrong? Is everything all right, child?" Liza was so anxious to tell, all she could say was, "Everything is more than all right. Berlin asked me to marry him. We're engaged." Estrada was so excited, she told everybody in the house at once.

Everybody was happy, except for Lance, her father. He said nothing; he just walked away as if Estrada said nothing. Liza spoke excitedly, "Ok! I have to get back to the prom. I'll see you when I get home." Before hanging up, Estrada told Liza how happy she was for her and to have a good time. They hung up, and Liza immediately began to think about the wedding.

Back inside the prom, the party was still jumping. Liza was pinching herself to see if this night was a dream, and it wasn't. Liza was really positive about her future now; being married to a Hamgorium came with perks.

That entire night was magical. Liza was still in shock from it all. They left the prom around eleven o'clock. With an hour to kill, they decided to grab a quick bite to eat. They stopped by the Dozier's place. Connie and Dexter sat at a booth together. Berlin and Liza sat at a separate booth and decided to set a date to get married. They chose to marry after graduating from college. Berlin began to talk about some items of importance and Liza agreed with everything. When she wanted to say something, he listened and agreed. It was eleven thirty. It was time for him to return Liza to her home. He dared not keep her out past curfew; he was too much of a gentleman for that.

On the ride home everyone was silent; nobody had anything to say. Liza just kept thinking, this is a dream and I'll wake up any minute. Berlin just sat and stared at his future wife. She was so beautiful, he couldn't keep his eyes off her. They drew closer together and kissed passionately. They didn't mind Dexter and Connie being there. The limo came to a stop, and so did they.

The chauffeur got out and opened the door for them. They all climbed out of the back seat. Berlin and Liza held hands all the way to the door. Estrada just couldn't wait for them to enter the house. As soon as she heard them on the porch, she ran to open the door. Hugging Berlin, she said, "I knew you were going to marry Liza." All the other soon to be in-laws hugged him as well, everybody except Lance. Everyone inside just stared at the rock on her finger, and the women made comments. Sage laughed, saying, "You need a dump truck to haul that hand around." Everyone laughed in agreement. Liza knew that her dad wasn't going to be happy about the engagement, and for his own sick reason, he felt he had every right to be angry. Berlin and Dexter didn't stay long. They were pretty beat. After they had left, Liza sat and told everyone how romantic it was the way he proposed to her.

Connie chimed in telling them how everyone in the gym went crazy over their engagement. They talked a little while longer.

Soon, it was 1:30 a.m. Liza and Connie, feeling sleepy, went upstairs to go to bed. Once they were up there, they got out of their fancy clothes and slipped on their pajamas. After washing the make-up off their faces, they crawled into bed. The girl's talked some more before falling asleep. It was 2:30 a.m., and they were off to dreamland. Liza was so anxious about where life was going and how fast, she awoke early. It was 5:00 a.m. She laid there for a minute before she awakened Connie.

"Hey Connie, wake up! I know you're sleeping, but I need to talk to you."

"All right Liza, I'm up. What's on your mind?"

"Connie, this is oh so sudden. I love Berlin and all, but this ... she ... paused. I am getting married in four years, and that's a big commitment. Yes, I'm ready to marry, even though I'm young. Connie, I know the things I want, and marriage is one of them."

Connie, being the good friend she was, laughed and said, "Liza, Berlin is the man for you. Both of you have been interested in each other since preschool. You can't find a relationship like the one you and Berlin have, Liza. Everything you guys are doing is great. Besides you guys are getting married after college. That's four years from now, so relax, it's going to be ok."

"I guess you're right, I'm worried about nothing. I just need to let life take its course and stop trying to predict it myself." On that note they fell back to sleep.

When they awakened, it was twelve noon. Connie jumped up in fear saying, "Oh my God, Liza, ... school! We're late for school."

"Girl, we're done with school, remember?"

"Oh! Yeah! That's right. We are through with school." There was no rush for them to get out of bed, so Liza turned on the television, with the volume on low. Liza, still a little nervous about her engagement, brought up the subject once again. Connie, being the good friend she is, listened. "Connie ... Berlin and I are getting married in September, four years from now. We will be going to college, and that will take four years to finish. I think I forgot to tell you. Berlin and I got a full scholarship to go to any top fashion design school in the country. Berlin will pick the college we'll attend. We're going to college in September so we can be finish in four years. You know with him picking the college, it will be the best." Connie was happy for Liza.

She smiled and said, "You guys are going to be so successful. Besides, Liza, you and Berlin don't have to work. If you guys decide to work, if you choose to, you can work at your family business. Heck, you two are the richest kids in town." They both giggled as Liza looked at her engagement ring in a daze.

Liza thought to herself. Ok, this is not a dream, this is real. She was afraid because she knew they were taking a big step. Even though they were young, they were still viewed as kids, but they loved each other. What they had was not puppy love, it was true love. They had known each other their entire lives and had been in a serious relationship since the ninth grade. Liza was still a virgin, so he thought, and so was Berlin, in a sense. The girls finally got out of bed. They cleaned themselves up and got dressed. They made sure the beds were made and the room was clean, and they headed downstairs.

Everyone was at the table eating breakfast, even though it was late in the afternoon. There were two plates there waiting for Liza and Connie. Once Liza sat down at the table, her dad got up and left. Everybody fell hushed. They were all puzzled by his behavior toward her. Liza said, "Well, pass me those waffles and bacon." They all began to talk about where Liza was going to college in two months. She told everyone of her plan. Although they both had rich parents, they were straight A+ honor students since the fourth grade by earning their honors. For two months Berlin and Liza searched for colleges to attend, and they found a college in Paris.

In August they both flew to Paris to enroll in their new school. They were excited about the adventure of being in a different country. Once they arrived at the college, they were entranced by its beauty. They couldn't wait to step inside. From the brochure, the college had a lot to offer. They stayed in Paris for two weeks to take care of business. They looked for two separate apartments; they didn't want to live together until they were married. They each found the perfect loft in the same building. Liza took the loft on the fifth floor, and Berlin took the one on the fourth floor. Ironically, Liza's was directly above Berlin's. After checking out their apartments, they went to the malls that were in the area. They wanted to know the area a little bit so when they returned they would have a general idea of their surroundings. The school was very prestigious, and the students were the snooty type. They thought they were better than others. Berlin and Liza decided to visit the clothing store on campus. It was the store that carried all the college students' designs. They were appalled at what they saw. A lot of the designs were tacky and prototypes of other designers, nothing original. They knew they had no competition at their new school. Their designs would steal the show. They were prepared to do just that. They knew there would be jealousy of what they could do. They were original. In fact, Liza and Berlin were coming there with their own designs. Perhaps it would make those students feel threatened, but Berlin and Liza didn't care; they were just being themselves. They were expecting to be called show-offs and arrogant asses. They were used to it anyhow. They never were show-offs; they were just good at what they did. They decided to take a tour around the area. They came upon a newsstand with tour maps. Liza grabbed one.

Chapter Two

The dark secret

Liza and Berlin headed back home the following morning. They each paid their security deposits and four months rent. They left Paris with their leases and their keys. They had a new life ahead of them, and they were both excited about it. The flight home was a smooth one. They had one month to get their stuff together back home. They agreed to spend a lot of time together with their two best friends, Connie and Dexter. They knew once they left for college, it would be a long time before they saw them again. They weren't coming home from college on vacation until Christmas.

Time flew by; it was time for them to head off to college in two weeks. Liza and her family went out to dinner to celebrate her new success in life. Her dad, Lance, wasn't present; he resented her leaving and her engagement. Liza didn't care though; she preferred he didn't come; he would have just spoiled it for everybody. Liza kept a secret. She made a promise to self that she would tell her mom before she left for college.

After dinner and arriving home, they all sat around relaxing from the outing. Liza knew she would tell her mom that night, but the time just wasn't right yet. Estrada made tea for everyone. That was her thing, tea and coffee.

That night some of her siblings turned in for the night earlier than usual. Sage, Keanu, and Liza were still awake. Lance was in the library having a drink. He had a feeling that one day Liza would tell, and he was right. He just didn't know when. It was 11:00 p.m. Liza took a sip of tea before clearing her throat. Estrada, looking her way, knew she was going to say something. Liza spoke, "Mom, may I speak to you alone please?" Estrada quickly arose to her feet saying, "Sure, let's go to the sun porch."

On the way there, Liza thought about how to tell her, but nothing seemed easy. Her mother, all smiles, walked in and sat down, waiting for Liza to say something. Liza, closing the door behind her, was worried about the outcome of what she was about to say. She knew she had to finally get it off her chest. Liza took a deep breath and paused before she spoke. Estrada knew it was important because of Liza's demeanor. "Mom, there is something I need to tell you. I should have told you when I was seven, but I was too afraid to tell you. Dad and Grandpa have been molesting me for eleven years. The last time Dad had sex with me was a month ago. Remember that day I came home and went to my room. I spoke to no one in this house for a week. That was the day he took me to a hotel and forced me to have sex with him. He even forced me to perform oral sex on him, too. If grandpa wasn't so sickly now, he would have been there, too. Do you want to know the last time grandpa molested me? It was two years ago. I was sixteen. After that, he was diagnosed with brain cancer. He was too ill to bother me anymore, and I was so glad he had brain cancer and was dying." With tears rolling down her face, her mother, in shock, yelled, "Shut up! You're a liar. Your dad and grandpa would have never done such a thing!"

"Listen, Mom. Why do you think Dad is so upset about my engagement? In his mind, I am only supposed to sleep with him and no one else." Estrada rose to her feet and slowly walked towards her with tears rolling down her face. Liza was expecting her mother to hold her and tell her that she was sorry. But she had a rude awakening coming. Once she was close enough to Liza, Estrada raised her hand and hit Liza so hard she stumbled. She yelled, "Get out of my house you lying heifer! You think because you're pretty you got men flocking! You always have been a tease and a flirt!"

When everyone heard all the commotion, they came running into the sun room. Liza screamed. "What? I get hit because your husband, my father, has a problem, and you're so stuck on having money that you overlook what he did to me! You're just as sick as he is!" She quickly left and headed to her room. Sage knew what was going on because she felt something wasn't right with her dad. She had some uncomfortable moments with him herself. He never made a move because Liza was still there. Sage followed behind her, calling her name. "Liza, slow down. I need to talk to you."

Once they were in her room, Liza slammed the door so hard it was heard all the way downstairs. She spoke in an angry voice. "Sage, this is why I never told Mom. I knew she wouldn't believe me. She always has thought that he was perfect." She paced the floor, angry that her mom slapped her that way. She began to pack all that was hers. She grabbed the bags that were packed for college along with six others. Liza and Sage headed toward the door. Liza said her goodbyes to her other siblings and exited the door. Sage asked, "Liza, where are you going?"

"I don't know Sage, somewhere. Look, I'll see you soon. Make sure you steer clear of dad. Love you! Bye!"

"I will, Liza, I know what happened, and I'm no dummy." Liza was crying so hard it made her ill. She called Berlin before she pulled off. "Berlin, it's me, Liza." He knew by her tone something was wrong.

"Liza, what's wrong, where are you?" She just sat in her car crying, saying, "Berlin, give me a minute; I'll call you back." She hung up. He was very alarmed. He called her phone, no answer.

Back inside, Estrada was angry. She was still crying over what just happened. Everyone was dying to know what had really gone on. Lance never came down from the library. He knew the bombs had exploded on his evil deed. Estrada went to the library, and there the bombs went off some more.

Liza had gotten her thoughts together and was able to call Berlin back. When his phone rang, he answered quickly. He asked once again, "Liza what's wrong? Where are you?" It took her a minute to gather her thoughts. She started the car and headed for the highway. Weeping, she began to tell him the horror story. Before she got into the story, he interrupted her asking, "Where are you going?"

"I don't know. My mom put me out. I'm going to get a room for two weeks, until we leave for college."

"No you're not. My parents bought me a house off the Bay in Tampa as a graduation present." She pulled alongside the road to get the address and directions. As she pulled over, he was still talking.

"You can stay there until we go, and I'll meet you there." She wrote the information down and headed back on the highway. She continued to tell him the story once she was back on the road. He listened. He grew angry, so he told her. "You have an hour drive. I'm driving, too, and I'm getting mad, so you can finish telling me in person." They hung up.

Liza knew that he was going to explode because it wasn't just her dad. It was her grandpa, too. She had an hour to get herself together so she could finish telling him. She reminded herself that she had done nothing wrong and that her mom needed to know what had been happening to her as a kid. Her thoughts were interrupted by the cell phone ringing. Looking at the caller ID, she answered. It was Sage on the other end saying, "Liza, what happened between you and

Mom?" Liza paused before answering. "Sage, try not to be alone with Dad. Right now you don't need to know why. You will soon." Sage spoke once more, frantically. "Mom and Dad are fighting. None of us down here knows what happened; all we know is that it's bad." Silence was the agenda now; she knew she couldn't tell Sage now. Liza let Sage know that she was fine and that she'll try to see them before she leaves. She dare not tell Sage where she was staying; she wanted no one to know. They ended their conversation with, I love you.

Liza had another thirty minutes to travel. She wished Sage hadn't called to question her. Liza was close to her destination. Back at Liza's parent's house, Estrada and Lance were still in a furious argument about Liza. All the kids could hear was, "You can't say it, can you? So there must be something to hide. No wonder you haven't been active with me, you've been too active with your own daughter." He just stood there looking at her snobbishly as if she was wrong for confronting him.

Estrada fled the house. She jumped in her car and headed to his dad's, Clyde's house. Sick over what had taken place, she pulled over on the next street and puked, disgusted with the whole thing. Her mind was spinning in so many directions, she thought she was going crazy.

Meanwhile, Liza made it to Berlin's block and searched for his address. She saw big, beautiful homes. She cruised down the street and spotted his address in the middle of the block. There was a big black iron gate before she could enter on to his property. She just drove right in, and the gate closed behind her. The house was on a few acres, so it was a drive to the house. Once she got closer to the mansion and the circular driveway, Berlin saw her on the security camera. Once he closed the gate, he walked to the balcony. She was in awe of the house. It was gorgeous, definitely a dream home. When she got out of the car, he whistled at her. He leaned over the railing, waiting for her to get close enough to catch her keys. When he threw them down to her, he said, "This is your home, too." Liza walked in and was greeted by a butler. "Good evening ma'am, may I take your things? Is there anything else out in the car? Sir Berlin is in the library." She couldn't believe her eyes; the house seemed larger on the inside than the outside. She stood there looking at the beautiful home. Berlin came down the stairs, walked up to her, gave her a big hug, and planted a kiss on her lips. He led her up to the T.V.

room. He sat her down and poured two glasses of white wine. They took a couple of sips and relaxed, holding each other. Berlin spoke, "Baby, you know it's going to be all right, I'm here for you." Tears welled up in her eyes. She reached for her cell phone to shut it off; she didn't want to be bothered with anyone tonight. He poured her another glass of wine. She took a sip and cleared her throat to talk. "So, as I was saying in the car. My dad has been molesting me since I was seven, and my grandpa has, too." Berlin flipped and yelled, "What? And what was your mom doing about it?"

"She did nothing." He drew close to Liza and held on to her. It was late. The butler had retrieved the rest of her things from the car. Berlin had something he wanted to show Liza before they headed to bed. Grabbing her by her hand, he led her to a room down the hall. There was a huge double door that stood before them. He flung them wide open. He left the lights off until they were inside the room. When the lights came on, there were four heavy duty sewing machines sitting in the middle of the large room, and six tables along the wall with six tabletop sewing machines on them. There were three doors in the room, and behind each door there were all kinds of material to make clothes. They had leather, denim, imported genuine mink, and cashmere silk. They were in all colors and styles. They had everything they needed to start a clothing line. Looking at Liza, he said, "This is all for us. This is our dream … all in this room." Liza hugged and kissed Berlin. Staring into his eyes, she whispered, "I love you Berlin Hamgorium."

"I love you too, Liza Dozier."

Leaving the room, he turned the lights off. He walked ahead, grabbing her close to him, and up a flight of stairs they went. It was a separate wing, but it was a part of the main house. The master bedroom had a huge walk-in closet. Liza noticed all her things were put away already; the butler knew just where to put them. Berlin turned on the television while Liza prepared for bed. She went to the drawer and grabbed her pajamas. Not ready to call it a night, they decided to have more wine. Walking down the hallway, Berlin met the butler, who wanted to check on them. "Will there be anything else, Sir Berlin?"

"No, Jason, that will be all for tonight." The butler headed to his room. He lived on the grounds as did some of the other workers. Berlin came back with a bottle of expensive white wine from Paris. He was so distraught over what Liza has told him, he made her stop because he wasn't ready to hear it all at once. He was going to continue it in bed.

Liza was in the shower, soaking up the hot water and relaxing. She just wanted to get past this moment. She knew that the conversation about her dad and grandpa wasn't over. It was one in the morning, but they had nothing to do tomorrow, so they could sleep in. Once she was out of the shower, she slid right into bed. Berlin had her glass of wine waiting. It was ice cold. Berlin went to take a shower himself. While he did that, Liza watched T.V. She was feeling good from all the wine, and she felt she could tell him now with ease. Berlin crawled into bed with Liza, shut the television off, leaving the lamp on. He gave her a look that said a million words while saying, "Liza, at some point we have to get through the whole conversation, and we should do it now. I'm ready to hear it all, no interruptions."

"Well, ok, here goes." She told Berlin the truth, from the beginning to the end. She told him of the talk with her mother that led to her being there with him tonight. Tears rolled down their faces; she had finally told him about her hidden family secret. He couldn't believe what he heard. Throwing his hands up with tears rolling down his face, he spoke firmly. "You mean to tell me ever since you were seven, your dad and grandpa have been molesting you?"

She nodded "Yes" in shame. "Liza, you never told anyone? Why not? You carried that with you for eleven years, all by yourself?" She nodded "Yes" and burst into tears. Berlin just held her tight, kissing her. He stopped slowly, looking into her eyes. He said, "Liza, baby, why didn't you tell me? I've known you since preschool and you never told me. But first and foremost, why didn't you tell your mom?"

"Because I was afraid no one would believe me, and I was right. My mom took his word over mine."

"Liza, I still can't fathom the thought of your mom allowing it." She shot back, "No, Berlin, you don't know my mom, she is money hungry. She'll put up with anything to have the money she has, even this. My dad has done some things to my mom that she should have left him for, but she stayed, for the money." Berlin angrily asked, "When was the last time it happened?" Looking down at the floor, she said, "It was two years ago with my grandfather, and my dad last month." Sick to his stomach, he ran to the bathroom and puked. Afterward, he brushed his teeth and washed his face and got himself together. When he came back, Liza was overwhelmed. She was staring in space, and he was blown away.

They laid there silently staring at the ceiling, wondering what the other was thinking. He began to think about her not being a virgin since she was seven, and that saddened him the most. They curled up together and began kissing. They were naked by now, and they began to caress. Before they knew it, they were making love. Liza finally had sex without force, and she loved it.

Estrada finally made it to Clyde's house. He was a rich old bastard that had twenty-four hour nursing service, all because he didn't want to go into hospice care. Although he was sick, he was able to move and talk. When he saw her face, he knew why she was there. He motioned the nurse to step out, so that he and Estrada could talk. His room was sound proof, so he wasn't worried about anyone hearing anything. She threw herself onto the chair that was next to his bed and said, "You better tell me something I want to hear, old man. Cause if it's what she told me, you and your son are dead." Looking at her, laughing, he said, "Shut up and listen, gal. That's your problem now, and it was then, too. You don't listen. That's why we were able to get away with it. I tell you Estrada, Liza is something special. Now that I know what you're here for, I'm going to give it to you. The answer to your question is, yes. We did everything she said, and it was fun, too. We had her before anyone ever could. Now, what are you going to do?" Estrada was enraged by what he just told her. She looked him in the eyes and said, "You better die, you son of a bitch, before I get back and do you in. You better hope and pray your boy makes it through the night." She stormed out of his room like nobody's business. She wanted to kill him right there on the spot, but she had to do it with class. She was upset by what he had said and done to Liza. Estrada realized she had ruined her relationship with her oldest daughter. But like Liza said, her mom was keeping her money, even though her husband earned it all. Estrada saw red. She knew her husband was a cheater, but not with his own flesh and blood.

Liza and Berlin were still going at it, but they were about to wrap it up. It was now 4:30 a.m., and they were both exhausted. They lay side by side breathing hard. They whispered, I love you, to each other and fell off to sleep.

When Berlin awakened, it was 10:00 a.m. He got out of bed without waking up Liza. He brushed his teeth and showered. Liza heard the water, woke up, and headed to the bathroom. She got in the shower with Berlin, kissing him all over. He was so glad that she was with him. She was wearing his ring proudly; she was ready to say I do today. They scrubbed each other's bodies, then rinsed. They were clean again. They both began to dry off. Looking at him in awe, she spoke, "You were awesome last night." He responded in that sexy monotone, "Really, so were you babe." They got dressed and headed down for breakfast.

Like kids in a candy store, they sprinted down the stairs. Berlin, smiling, felt good because he wasn't the only one with a secret, but his secret wasn't to be told to her yet. He said, "We're eating on the deck off the bay." When they went past the kitchen, the chef was already preparing breakfast. Looking at his boss with a smile, he said, "Breakfast will be served in fifteen minutes, sir, and there is a cart waiting to take you and the lovely lady down to the bay." Nodding his head in approval he said, "Very good, Jack, can you prepare a tray of fresh fruit?"

"It's already done, sir." He smiled and walked towards the cart with Liza in tow. They said nothing on the way up. They just enjoyed the view. There was an enclosed deck off the bay. Liza asked, "This isn't a part of your property, is it?"

"Yes it is. My dad had this built two years ago. At first this was just the bay leading to our land, then he had this roadway done out here."

"Wow! That's interesting."

"Here comes the chef with our breakfast. I hope you like the food." Before he reached them, Berlin spoke quickly. "Liza, after breakfast we need to go see my parents to tell them what happened. They can help." Uncomfortable with it, she said, "No, I'm not ready to tell anyone else."

"You don't have to, I'll tell it." She agreed. Placing the trays in front of them, everything looked delicious. They enjoyed every bite. The cart was parked up the hill. They sat for a minute so their food could settle before they headed to the house.

Back at the house, Liza checked the mirror once more. She applied some makeup to look her best, as usual. Grabbing her purse, she was ready to do this. Once they were in the car, Berlin spoke. "Liza, there's something I need to tell you. I didn't tell you last night because of all that was going on. But, I put your name on the deed once my parents gave me the house. Our names are the only ones on the deed. On the deed it says Liza Hamgorium because I know you are going to be my wife." She was speechless. She just sat and stared straight ahead. He knew she was floored, so he just let her savor the moment.

They had an hour drive to his parent's house, but that wasn't too bad. They were there in no time. Liza was nervous about what they would think of her now. There wasn't a need to knock, he had a key, and they just walked in. Berlin's parents, Kumar and Asti, were glad to see them. They embraced Liza like a daughter as they always have. Asti had tea waiting for them in the dining hall. It was called a hall because it was huge and they held a lot of dance balls there. Once they sat and were comfortable, Berlin began to talk.

"Mom, Dad. What I'm about to tell you will be shocking, so please don't look at Liza any differently." His parents looked at each other and motioned for him to continue. He told them the exact same thing Liza told him. Every time she heard that story, she felt nasty and dirty. His parents were at first apprehensive about believing that. They didn't know what to say. They just sympathized with her and then asked questions. They stayed for dinner and no more was spoken about Liza's problem.

After dinner, Asti called Estrada to see if what was spoken of was true. Asti spoke nothing of Liza at first. But oh, it changed when Asti asked about it and

Estrada said it was true. It really infuriated Asti when she asked Estrada what she was going to do about it. She had no response. Asti hung up and told Kumar it was true what Berlin told them. They were floored by the whole thing; they felt so bad for Liza. They told her they were sorry about what happened to her and they would help her any way they could. She was glad to hear that she wasn't out here alone, because her mom wasn't a line of support. Only her siblings were.

They had a couple more glasses of wine and talked a while longer. Berlin looked at his watch and said, "Well, Mom and Dad, Liza and I should leave. It's been stressful for her these last couple of days. We're going to go home so she can rest."

"All right, son. Make sure you call on that account Monday."

"Ok, will do, Dad. Don't forget to move the funds Monday morning from the payment we received from the big account we just landed." Nodding his head, he and Asti got up and saw them to the door. Once they got to the door, Asti grabbed and hugged Liza tight and said, "We love you very much. Take care of yourself. We're here for you, dear." Kissing her on the cheek, Liza said, "Thanks. I love you Mom and Dad." She felt better after her visit with her soon to be in-laws. She smiled while walking to the car. Berlin was so ecstatic to see her smile, he just smiled along with her without saying a word. He opened the car door for her as a gentleman would. She put on her seatbelt and sat comfortably in her seat. They said nothing on the way home; they just listened to music all the way there.

They arrived home around ten o'clock at night. They were both full from dinner at his parent's house, and they were good on the wine, too. They just wanted to shower, put on their pajamas, and lounge in bed the rest of the night. Liza showered first; she didn't take long because she was tired. Berlin didn't take long either. They settled in bed with the television on. They popped the movie *Ghost Rider* into the DVD player.

Once the movie was over, they decided to talk. Liza didn't know what to say, but Berlin did. Turning on his back he said, "You know, Liza, they need to pay for what they have done to you, they can't just get away with it."

"How are they supposed to pay, Berlin?"
He gave her a look she had never seen before. Knowing what he was going to say, she covered his mouth before he could speak. She interrupted his thought saying, "No, Berlin, that would just kill my

mother if you did that." He sat in silence, because he knew Liza would be hurt again by his actions toward her father and grandfather. Liza just wanted to sleep, among other things. Once again, before they would go to sleep, they engaged in hot, steamy love-making. Falling asleep afterwards was their thing, and they did just that.

Berlin had awakened by 9:00 a.m. He already knew Jack, his chef, was preparing breakfast. Without waking Liza, he crawled out of bed and made his way to the bathroom. He brushed his teeth, took a shower, and headed downstairs. Just as he was walking into the kitchen, Jack was making him a cup of coffee. Jason was packing all his things for college. Liza had to go to her parents to pick up some more of her things. Liza slept until nine-thirty. She woke up refreshed and feeling better because of her restful night. She smelled breakfast, headed for the bathroom, and showered.

She felt like a new woman. Making her way down to the kitchen, she clipped her cell phone to her side. She had a smile on her face as she entered the kitchen, as did Berlin. Every time he saw her, his face lit up the entire room. He believed in greeting a woman when she entered the room, so he was prepared to do so. "Good morning, babe, how did you sleep?"

"Wonderfully, I slept like a baby."

"That's great, I'm glad to hear that. Well, Jack has prepared our breakfast, and coffee is in the dining hall." Liza stood there looking at Berlin with a smile on her face. Realizing she hadn't seen the entire house, he decided to lead her on a tour after breakfast. Jason, the butler, came in and placed their plates in front of them. They thanked him and began to eat breakfast.

They talked about leaving for college in three weeks. They were excited, but things had to change in their lives and there were some things to be talked about. Berlin spoke first, "Liza, we both know that things have changed since our prom night, and there are some things we need to look at."

"The first order of business should be your apartment. There is no sense in paying a lease on two places. Your place has three bedrooms, so I suggest we stay in yours and get a refund on mine. Once we get the money back for the deposit on my place, we'll put it on your place. That way we are covered for the one year we'll be there." Liza was pleased to hear that she wouldn't be alone and said, "Berlin, that's a great idea. There was no need to say anything else because they knew it was all going to work out. Liza wondered if Berlin thought any different of her, but he didn't. He still viewed her as a virgin, because her virginity was taken away from her against her will. Berlin asked, "What do you say we view the house today? I'll show you every inch of it."

"I'd like that very much. How many bedrooms are in here?"

"There are nine bedrooms and seven bathrooms. This house has a flower and vegetable garden, it is loaded with space. It has a tennis court, indoor and outdoor pool, library, recreation room, music room, and a sauna. It sits on seven acres and has three guest cottages on the premises. Yes, this is a mansion my love." Liza's heart stopped, she couldn't believe she was living in such a lavish home.

They took their last bite and began the tour. First they went into the kitchen; it was a restaurant style kitchen with all the new amenities. He opened the door that led to the chef's pantry, filled with food. He opened another door, hit the switch, and down the stairs they went. It was like the rest of the house- beautiful and spotless. Liza was shocked by all the exercise equipment, at least fifty thousand dollars worth. They went across the hall to another room.

"This is the recreation room; it has seven arcade games, a pool/ping pong table, and a built in television with a complete top-of-the-line sound system." The music room was around the corner. They walked through a long corridor and up six steps to the garden outside. They walked four acres. From where they were Liza could see the cottages and the pool. Soon they came upon a five car garage. He opened the door, and inside there were five vehicles, and all of them were 2011 Mustangs. He threw her the keys, and said, "This is yours. I bought you a mustang that matches mine for your graduation. Congratulations on graduating." Liza was in awe over the present he just gave her; she just wanted to cry. She loved every bit of the house and the grounds it was on. It had the most beautiful landscaping she'd ever seen. The flower garden had colorful flowers and stones and a wishing pond in the middle. They kept heading toward the house. They looked at each other and took off running. They were racing to the house. Half way there, they stopped and rolled in the grass. They landed in each other's arms and kissed. They rolled and rolled until they were dizzy. They gazed into each other's eyes, rose to their feet, and walked the rest of the way home. Jack had lemonade waiting for them inside. Berlin began to show her the remainder of the house. By the end of the tour, Liza couldn't believe how beautiful the home was. Heading to the movie theater, they grabbed their 3D glasses to watch a movie. Jack knew they were doing movies today because he checked Berlin's daily agenda. Once they were settled in their seats, Jason came in to take their order for the movies. Popcorn and nachos it was, along with the lemonade Jack had made fresh. Liza all of a sudden felt ill. She just wanted to lie down. Berlin canceled the movie but kept the order in. He walked Liza up to their room. Placing her in the king size bed, she just laid there.

Before long, she had to run to the bathroom. Stuffing her head down in the toilet, she vomited. She was getting worried because it was rare when she was sick. After her date with the porcelain bowl, she wanted to shower. Berlin grabbed a pair of pajamas for her to wear. Liza found it hard to stand there and brush her teeth. Her stomach was still in knots. Rinsing her mouth out almost caused her to repeat her visit to the porcelain bowl, but it didn't happen. She was finally able to make her way into the shower. She stood there and soaked up all the water, letting it beat down on her head and back. She stayed there for at least a half an hour. She felt so much better afterwards.

Liza was thinking she had to get it together because they were leaving for school in three weeks. At least they didn't have to pack; that was already done by their family members.

Back at Liza's house things were quiet, but scary. Estrada had not a word for her husband, Lance, and all she could think about was how to knock his father off without being blamed for his untimely death. The old slime ball had only a year, but Estrada wanted him to go now. Keanu, Liza's favorite sister, was debating if she should give Liza a call, so she picked up the phone and dialed the house number. Liza picked up and answered.

"Hello."

"Hey Liza, how are you doing?"

"Keanu, how are you? I was thinking about you just a minute ago."

"I'm good Liza, but it's not the same with you being gone."

"Yeah, I know, but it's all right, I'm good."

"Well, that's good to hear. So you're leaving in three weeks for college. I wish you well, Liza, I do. I know you're just going to wow them there, you and Berlin. Oh! By the way, tell him I said hi. But I called you to see if you want to hook up tomorrow, just us siblings, no Mom or Dad."

"That would be nice, you can all drive up here to the house, and I'll have Jack prepare dinner."

"Who is Jack?"

"Jack is our chef, and Jason is our butler."

"Liza girl, I see what you mean; you are living better there than you were here!"

"I sure am, but I have to go now, I haven't been feeling good for the past few hours."

Jason was on his way in the room just as she hung up the phone. She quickly ran to the bathroom once the smell of the food hit her nose. After vomiting, she cleaned her mouth and face. She told Berlin, "The smell of food, I can't take it." Looking at her, he didn't know what to say.

They had only three weeks to go before they were leaving. Liza figured she'd better get a checkup before leaving. Berlin was thinking the same thing. She made an appointment for after the weekend to find out what was going on with her.

Later that night Liza called Keanu to tell her that she wanted them to come over next Saturday. Keanu understood because she knew Liza was ill. It was Thursday and Liza's appointment was Tuesday. She planned to rest in bed and eat a lot of soup to fight off what her illness was. The days flew by. Before they knew it, it was Monday. Still, everything that smelled like food made her ill. Neither Liza nor Berlin could make sense of it all; they both were anxious to get her checked out. Liza laid around all day that day, staying clear of the kitchen area. All she wanted was to get better so she could prepare for college.

Berlin went about business that day. He knew he had to work to get the bills paid. The family business was a successful one; his family owned a very large accounting firm. Kings and Queens were clients of theirs, and his mom owned her own clothing store. In that store she had her own clothes she designed and sewed. Berlin was part owner in the company, and he worked in the firm. He brought a lot of business to the firm and closed some big accounts. He didn't stay at work very long because he knew Liza was home ill. He worked five hours and went home. It was now two in the afternoon.

Once he was home, he asked Jack to make Liza some homemade chicken soup. Carrying it upstairs to her, he let her know he was coming in with it. Sipping on her orange juice that Jack made freshly squeezed, she let Berlin know it was okay to come in. She grabbed the soup immediately after Berlin placed it on the T.V. tray, taking a sip of it. She lay back in bed with a soothing look on her face, saying, "That feels so good for my stomach." Berlin said, with a smile, "I hope you can eat all of it. You'll get better."

Rising from the bed, she sat up and continued to eat her soup. Finishing her orange juice, Berlin poured her some more. Looking at the clock, she had an hour before her show, *House,* came on. She headed toward the shower with a pair of pajamas. She soaked under the water for twenty minutes before washing her hair. She used top-of-the-line body scrub, so she was going to be smelling good. Leaving the bathroom steamy, Berlin headed in to take his shower so he could relax in bed with Liza the rest of the evening. They both fell asleep around midnight.

When they awakened, it was 8:00 a.m. Liza's doctor appointment wasn't until 10:00 a.m. Getting their hygiene together, they had enough time to have coffee and breakfast.

During the ride to the doctor they talked about college and what they planned to do once they were there. They laughed and talked all the way. After entering the doctor's office, Liza began to dig for her ID and her insurance card. Reaching the registration desk, she signed in. The nurse gave her a clipboard with the forms needed to check her in. The form took her twenty minutes to fill out. She signed the back of the form and handed it over to the desk clerk.

Waiting patiently for the medical assistant to call her, she chose a magazine to read. They were finally called. Berlin stayed behind in the waiting room. After the medical assistant weighed Liza, she took her to a room to take her vital signs. She waited in the room for thirty minutes, twiddling her fingers. She heard a knock at the door, and then the door opened. "Hello, my name is Dr. Ash. I will be examining you today." He asked her some questions and began his tests. He gave her a cup to urinate in and ordered blood work and a pregnancy test. He told her to wait in the waiting room for the results of the pregnancy test. She told Berlin about the pregnancy test. He was nervous, and so was Liza. The test results would take thirty minutes. Berlin began to pace the floor. Just as he began to pace, the medical assistant called both of them back to the room Liza just left. They waited for the doctor to return with the results. He arrived within minutes. He looked at the results and told them they were going to be parents. They sat stunned, staring in space. After the shock wore off, they began to smile.

They were happy about the baby, but still shocked by it. Before leaving the room, the doctor gave Liza a prescription for prenatal vitamins and folic acid. The doctor explained to them that Liza had been experiencing morning sickness. He also told her it would pass and that she was two weeks pregnant. Gathering up all the pamphlets that were given to her, she had her appointment set for the following month. Before they left, she explained to the doctor about their change of resident and asked if he could recommend an obstetrician in Paris. The doctor wrote a note to his nurse, and she began to search immediately. They would be given names of doctors in a day or so. They left the office.

Once they were in the car, they had to sit for a minute. They still couldn't believe the pregnancy. Berlin started the car, kissed Liza softly on the cheek, and began driving. Liza was silent in thought. She knew she could take two extra classes and graduate in one year. They talked about it on the way home and decided they would both take the extra classes. Now they were thinking how to tell the family, but Berlin was thinking of more. Silence was between them for the remainder of the ride home. Exhausted from all the activity, Liza just wanted to rest. Berlin ordered tuna salad and tea for each of them.

Liza and Berlin headed to the shower. Showering together, Berlin rubbed Liza's belly the entire time. After drying and dressing, Jack entered with their order. Liza gulped down her food; she was starved. She ordered seconds. Berlin spoke, "Liza, I know we discussed marriage. We said in two years, but now you're pregnant, and now is perfect." Liza agreed. With a smile on his face, he spoke again. "Here's what we'll do. I'll call the pastor tomorrow. I'll call my parents, and you can call your family. Oh yeah! Don't forget Dexter and Connie. How's three days sound?" She agreed. Looking at her phone, she noticed she had four missed calls from her mom's house. She called back, and her mom answered. Liza said drily, "Hello Mom." Estrada, clearing her throat, spoke quickly. "Liza, I know the truth, and I just want to apologize for calling you a liar."Liza was glad to hear that, but she knew her mom wasn't going to leave her dad. She decided to tell her mom that she and Berlin were getting married in three days. Screaming for joy, Estrada ran through the house telling everybody. Liza hung up the phone with a smile on her face. Berlin expressed his thoughts about not wanting to see her mother, but that he understood that Estrada is their child's grandmother. Liza explained to him what just transpired between her and her mother. She told him about the heartfelt apology and her acceptance of the apology. Berlin was all right with it, but he wanted to know what Estrada was going to do about it. Berlin told Liza that the time was set for two o'clock, and the reception would be catered. The plan was to wake tomorrow, go get the wedding gown, his ring, and the tuxedo.

The morning of the wedding Liza went to the hair salon and the spa. She was beautiful for her soon-to-be husband. Those three days came quickly. Soon she was walking down the aisle about to become a Hamgorium. There were at least two hundred people-amazing on such short notice. Their families were popular. Liza was glad her dad didn't show up, and she knew her grandpa wasn't going to be there either. As she was walking down the aisle, she noticed how handsome Berlin looked standing there. She read his lips saying, "You look beautiful." A tear rolled down her cheek. She was so happy. The wedding went off perfectly, no flaws. She was no longer Liza Dozier. She was now Liza Hamgorium. The wedding reception was just as beautiful as the wedding. Everyone had a great time. Liza and Berlin got up on the stage and made their announcement. Everyone silently waited. Liza spoke. "First, I would like to thank all of you for coming out tonight, sharing in this wonderful ceremony on such short notice. I also want to thank you for the gifts. We also want to share some exciting news; Berlin and I are having a baby." The grandparents jumped for joy, and so did Liza's siblings. They were so happy. Berlin spoke, "We went to the doctor three days ago. That's when we found out we were going to be parents. Liza is two weeks pregnant, and she is healthy. Everyone clapped. Please continue to enjoy the rest of the night, and have a good time." Stepping down from the stage, Liza's mom and siblings, along with Berlin's parents, surrounded both of them, hugging and kissing each other and congratulating them on their new arrival. Time went by. The hired cleaners began to clean the facility, and the guests began leaving. Liza and Berlin left thirty minutes before. The butlers hauled all their wedding gifts to the van to bring to their house.

When the butlers arrived with the gifts, Berlin and Liza were in their pajamas drinking tea in the family room. Once all the gifts were inside, they began to open some of them. They were growing tired from the long day, so they decided to open the rest of the gifts when they returned from their honeymoon. They were leaving the next day for the Virgin Islands and would return in five days. That would leave them a week and five days to come home and prepare to leave for college. They rested for their flight; it was leaving at five in the morning. Berlin was happy to be a married man, and Liza was the happy wife. Berlin turned off the television, and they began to kiss. Tonight was the night they were going to consummate their marriage. That night was special. They were no longer making love as fiancées; they were now husband and wife. They loved every moment of the closeness and passion with each other. Liza knew what love truly was at that moment. It was different from all the other times she and Berlin made love.

Liza and Berlin fell asleep, waking at three in the morning. Liza called and canceled the hold on Berlin's apartment in Paris. She explained to the manager that they got married and would be moving into her apartment. The manager remembered them. Liza told the manager to put the two thousand dollar deposit from Berlin's apartment on hers. Everything was in order for them to go to college. Berlin took a shower. Liza picked out the clothes she was wearing to leave for their flight. Jason had already packed their luggage for their honeymoon, so they were all set to go. It was now four in the morning. Their flight was leaving at five. They were seated on the plane a half hour before the others. There flight was a lengthy one. With one lay over, only an hour. They were good with that because it gave them a chance to stretch and walk around. They used the restroom and grabbed some snacks. Although they were in first class, they preferred certain things they just didn't have on the plane. Boarding back on the plane, they settled into their seats. Six hours later they landed in the Virgin Islands. Once they arrived at their villa, they checked into their room. Dropping their bags off, they headed out to have fun. There was a lot to do, and they did everything. They had a wonderful time on the island.

On the flight back home to their first stop, they were so exhausted, they slept the entire time. They were awakened when they landed to board the next flight home. Once they were settled on the plane, they fell asleep again. Their driver was waiting for them when they got off the plane. Grabbing their luggage, the driver greeted them. "Hello sir, madam. How was your trip?" They greeted him kindly, telling him all about it.

Back at home, they were preparing for their flight to Paris, for college. They were both ready and knew they were making the right choice by going to fashion designing school. They had been designing clothes for years. They had already hired someone to decorate the nursery for the baby in Paris. It had to be a neutral color; they didn't know if it was a boy or a girl. All the loose ends were tied, they were ready to go. Liza, Berlin, and their families gathered for dinner at their favorite restaurant, Liza's parents' place. Her father didn't show up, and Liza was glad of that, but her siblings and mom came. That was the happiest day for everyone. They wished Liza and Berlin good luck on their journey. They were pleased that their family was so supportive. Leaving the restaurant, they all kissed and hugged, and they ended it with a prayer. They were ready and focused on college. They weren't concerned about the classes at all; they had confidence they would graduate with ease.

The next day, they hung out with Dexter and Connie. They went for dinner and bowling. After their night out, they all headed back to Berlin and Liza's house. Dexter and Connie knew it would be a long time before they would see Berlin and Liza. They all stayed up late and reminisced about all the crazy things done as kids together. They were laughing and talking, having a good time. Dexter had them rolling when he told the story about Berlin and him getting busted for smoking cigarettes. The girls laughed so hard, they almost peed their pants. Liza, still laughing, spoke, "I remember that, and your mom made you both clean the elderly's homes in the neighborhood for free.

The next morning, Liza sat in the enclosed sun porch smoking a cigarette, relaxing. This would be the last one because she was pregnant now.

Chapter three

A new life

There they were, in college, on their own. College was simple to them, but they still enjoyed it. Liza and Berlin stayed focused on their classes. They didn't hang out and party like most of the kids did. They had maintained their four point zero grade point average. The professors were blown away by them. Berlin and Liza showed the professors designs that no one had ever seen before. Even though they were both doing well in their classes, they were still trying to adjust to becoming parents, let alone being pregnant during college.

It was now December, and Liza was showing big time. She had been in school since August. The baby was due the end of March, first week of April. Liza decided to pick up one more class so she would have one more semester verses two to complete after giving birth. Berlin kept his classes as they were. They didn't feel like taking the flight home for Christmas because Liza was huge. She was healthy and so was the baby.

They made a videotape of her development over those four months and mailed a copy to both of their parents.

Excited about the baby and the upcoming school year, time was going by. Liza and Berlin had finished one semester. It was now January, and classes were back in full force. Liza was much bigger now; she was due in two months. They were concerned whether she would be able to make it until March in school. Berlin had to help her to her classes every day. He decided to hire a nurse's assistant to wheel her to class so she didn't have to walk so far.

Once March hit, she went on maternity leave from school. Everyone was so excited. The sex of the baby wasn't known as they wanted it to be a surprise. Berlin took a two week vacation during Liza's due date.

Late that night of March twenty-fifth, Liza and Berlin were getting ready for bed when Liza's water broke. Berlin, really excited, called an ambulance. The pain was excruciating for Liza. The ambulance finally arrived. The workers lifted her onto the gurney, and took her vitals. Berlin, right by her side, called home to let the rest of the family know that Liza was in labor. They were overjoyed and couldn't wait for the call back on whether it was a girl or a boy. The ride to the hospital wasn't long, but Liza was screaming in pain. All she wanted was to have that baby, "Now!"

After arriving at the hospital, they wheeled her to the back, checking her to see if she was crowning. They scrubbed up quickly and rolled her into one of the private delivery rooms. The nurse ordered Berlin to quickly scrub and get dressed in sterilized clothing, so he could be in there with her. Just as he was walking in, Liza was pushing for the first time, yelling, "Oh my God, I want to push some more." But, she was instructed to stop pushing. After the doctor untangled the umbilical cord, he instructed her to push again. This time when she pushed, the baby's head emerged. She was told to push harder this time. Taking a deep breath, she pushed really hard. When she did that, the entire body of the baby came out. After cutting the cord, he wrapped the baby up in a receiving blanket and suctioned her mouth. Holding her upside down, they smacked the baby on the butt to make it cry, and it did. Wiping off the baby, he handed it over to the parents. The doctor smiled and said, "Congratulations, it's a girl." Liza and Berlin were smiling from ear to ear. They were happy because the baby was healthy. Liza was so tired from the delivery, all she wanted to do was get some sleep. The baby had to be taken to the nursery to bathe, have tests run, and to get immunized. Berlin kissed Liza on the forehead and said, "Thank you for giving me a baby, Liza. You were wonderful. I'm going to go call the family and tell them it's a girl."

After the call, he headed back inside with Liza. She was sound asleep. He decided to go home and rest. He kissed her on the forehead once more and left. He couldn't wait to go back to see Liza and their beautiful daughter. The alarm went off at five thirty, and Berlin was up. He ate breakfast, drank coffee, and read the paper, waiting for visiting hours to start. 7:30 a.m. he jumped in their newly purchased Mercedes Benz and headed to the hospital.

When he arrived, Liza and the baby were together. Liza was watching television and feeding the baby. Berlin kissed Liza and the baby gently on their heads and cheek, and he grabbed and held his daughter in his arms, rocking her back and forth. He was so ready for fatherhood. The baby was beautiful, just like her mother. They named her London Marie Hamgorium. Liza and the baby had a short stay in the hospital. On the third day they were discharged and sent home. Everything was in order at home for the baby. The nursery was completed and all her furnishings were up. All three of the grandparents were there when Berlin arrived with Liza and the baby. The plan was for the grandmothers to stay with Liza and the baby for two weeks so Liza could rest. She had no idea the parents were there.

She was returning to school in four weeks. Berlin was looking for a nanny for London, once he and Liza started back to school. Berlin had two years left in college, while Liza had one and a half. They were allowed a two week leave of absence before spring break, which gave them an extra week and a half break.

Spring break was due to start in two weeks. That gave them plenty of time to hire a nanny for London. They enjoyed their lives as parents so far. Berlin and Liza loved her so much. They hated the fact that they had to return to school and leave London with a nanny, but it was worth it, they had big contracts waiting for them upon graduation. One contract was a multimillion dollar deal, with the first payment kicking in as soon as Liza graduated. They were already worth millions, but they were about to become worth much, much more.

Spring break came and went. Berlin decided he would take extra classes so he could graduate in a year verses two. He would graduate in the time allotted for the classes. Liza was graduating in August because she had taken three extra classes before her maternity leave. Liza was on a roll; it was now July. She had one more month before she would graduate.

They purchased a building and moved all of their machines and material there. They were ready for business. Everything was moved from Florida to Paris, still intact. Their business couldn't officially open until one of them had a license. Liza was graduating in one month, so they would be able to open their store. Berlin was going to work in the store. The name of their business was registered. They were going to get insured. The building was already insured. They had a building permit to remodel. After Liza graduated, they began the hiring process, looking over applications. It took them a couple of weeks to hire as many as twelve people. Liza took a month off before opening the store. She stayed home, made clothes, and took London out to spend time with her. London loved her mom being home, but was with the nanny most of the time. She didn't mind it because she loved her nanny. Liza and Berlin began to plan their grand opening to launch their Hamgorium Gear.

Everyone was waiting for their clothing line to hit the streets. Liza was glad the school part was over, as she and Berlin had difficulties with some of the other students. They had some haters throughout their entire time there.

CHAPTER FOUR

In business

5 years later

Liza and Berlin graduated from college with their fashion degrees. Their business has been booming for five years. They both ran the business while raising their five daughters. They were called the Hamgorium girls by everyone. From the oldest to the youngest, they were: London, Lahti, Leann, Lana, and Latasha. They were all drop-dead gorgeous like their mom. The girls were cared for by the nannies while their parents worked.

Liza and Berlin were on the cover of many magazines, and they were worth millions on top of millions. They made the blue blood magazines, the magazines that only the rich folks read. African American men and women all over the world never knew it was possible to be so rich. Liza and Berlin were, and race didn't matter. They had accounts to design clothes for Kings and Queens. Hamgorium Gear was global. It seemed every little girl, boy, and adult wore Hamgorium Gear. People loved their designs.

Liza and Berlin hadn't been home to Florida in five years, so they were due a vacation. They had faithful, trustworthy employees who could keep things running while they were gone. The company was doing extremely well. They weren't due to go back on tour with new designs until the following year. It was May 2009.

June came and they decided to go home. They tied up their loose ends, called, and made reservations for Florida. Before leaving, they made sure the books were straight and the inventory and profit margins were correct. Those two days flew by; it was time to go home. The girls were excited to meet their grandparents in person. London remembered them because she was the oldest. The other four were babies. The girls were six, five, four, three, and two. Liza had them a year apart.

They boarded their private jet and headed home to Tampa. No one knew they were coming; Liza and Berlin were surprising everyone. They were staying one week and would return for Thanksgiving and Christmas. The girls ran through the home they didn't know they had. Jack and the other staff at the house were glad to see them and were blown away by the Hamgorium girls. Yes, they heard about the girls and saw pictures, but they were even more gorgeous in person. The girls found their own way through the house, looking in every nook and cranny.

Liza ordered Jack to prepare a feast. She told Jason to her call their friends, Dexter and Connie. Berlin called his mom, Liza's mom, and her siblings. They all headed to their home. As Estrada and the others were leaving, Lance put on his hat and began to walk toward the door saying, "I'll drive." Estrada looked him up and down and said, "Oh no you're not; you won't be anywhere near Liza and those kids. You better be glad you and your sorry daddy are still alive," slamming the door behind her. She couldn't believe that old bastard was still alive with brain cancer, when he was supposed to have been dead five years ago.

Everyone arrived at Liza and Berlin's house. They were so glad to see the seven of them, especially the Hamgorium girls. Liza's siblings were seeing their nieces for the first time. They couldn't believe how the girls looked exactly like Liza. They had her perfect chocolate skin with her matching chocolate eyes and her long, black, wavy hair. Jack was in the kitchen preparing dinner. It would take at least two hours for him to prepare it all, but he was quick. The aroma of his cooking filled every room. Berlin closed his eyes and inhaled deeply. He missed that smell so much. He excused himself and headed to the kitchen with a smile on his face. Jack noticed him, continued cooking, and said, "Sir, I prepared your favorite dish for dinner tonight." Berlin, smiling, said, "Oooh! What is that Jack?"

"Beef ribs, some macaroni and cheese, I cooked greens, potato salad, and corn bread. For dessert, we're having strawberry cheese cake." Berlin walked over to the stove and leaned into the oven to see the ribs roasting. They looked delicious. That was one thing Berlin missed, Jack's cooking.

Walking through the house to see how well the staff had kept up the property was pleasing to Berlin. They had the remodeling done that Liza and Berlin requested before leaving for college. They had new furniture delivered, including bedroom sets for the girls delivered last year. It was so wonderful seeing everyone Berlin thought about while he was away. They were all seated in the family room talking. The kids were getting along well. Estrada was happy but quiet, doing some heavy thinking. She knew she had to take care of that problem. She finally decided to do it.

She knew Liza and her brothers and sisters would be fine. Snapping out of it, Estrada joined in the talking and laughing.

Dinner was served, and they headed for the dining hall. There sat a lavish twenty seat table. There was plenty of room for everyone. Jack, Jason, and Colleen served everyone. After they had served everyone, Berlin and Liza asked them to sit and eat with them, and they did. Everyone went to bed early that night because they planned a family outing to Disneyland. Asti had taken care of the reservations, and they all pitched in for it. They were staying three days. They planned several outings. On one of their outings, they visited Berlin and Liza's store to shop, their treat. People came in droves for autographs when they found out Berlin and Liza were at their store. They allowed a few people in, but once it got too crazy, they cut off the autograph session. Their family got a kick out of seeing them as famous, and they loved it. They all knew they were going to be famous designers; they were both too good not to be successful. Before long, it was time to go home and go back to work. They weren't looking forward to the flight home. Nevertheless, they were ready to go back to work. They were anxious to get back to the warehouse to make more of the designs that made them rich and famous. Dexter, Connie, and their children left two days before Berlin, Liza, and their kids were leaving. Asti, Kumar, and Estrada stayed until the day Liza, Berlin, and the kids left.

That morning, Berlin, Liza, the girls, the bodyguards, and the nannies headed back to Paris. They left on a Thursday but didn't arrive until Friday night.

Once they were home, Liza bathed the girls and put them to bed. Soon she showered and went to bed. Berlin stayed up and went over the books to see how much money was made while they were gone. He also looked over the application of a designer named Jean Dilbert. They were looking for another designer to help them design and sew their designs. Liza and Berlin interviewed Jean and a couple of other designers, but they chose Jean. He was self-motivated and an excellent designer; he was perfect. The business grew even more with Jean on board. He brought in some really high-priced clients. He had his fashion shows out of state, and he could bring big money into the Hamgorium gear company. Berlin and Liza were laid back; their company was paying for itself. They had a total of seventeen stores and twelve properties, eight of them lavish estates on ten acres or more. They lived in one of them. They were living high – on – the - hog. They didn't want for anything and neither did their children. They were happy where they were in life, and they were grateful for it all.

Time had gone by and they were still the top designers in the market. Jean was still with their company, and they added one more store to their establishment. They became a corporation now. Liza saw no end to their empire, but she was to be surprised at the changes that would come with it.

CHAPTER FIVE

The payback

Twenty five years had passed. Liza was now fifty years old. All of her daughters were married with two children apiece and had successful careers. Berlin and Liza were still married, but their relationship was different. Liza was still an attractive, flawless appearing woman. Berlin paid no attention to her and hadn't done so in the past eleven years. Liza, tired of his ignoring her, sought relations elsewhere. The men she was seeing were glad to be in a relationship with her, but they were all married men. Liza's daughters were concerned about their parents' marriage because they saw the change. But they left it up to them to repair it; they didn't want to intervene.

Years of the same behavior had gone on between Liza and Berlin. Berlin knew Liza was cheating, but he didn't care because he was also having an affair, for the past eleven years. Liza also knew Berlin was cheating, but she didn't know with whom.

Berlin began to stay nights away from home, and Liza began to have her rendezvous at home. The men she was seeing would visit her just before their wives were going to work. Merck and Bronze were her two favorite affairs. She was in love with those two. She was also seeing Michael, John, and Philip. Liza was on the wild. Her husband's rejection did a job on her mind. She had begun to think she was unattractive. Having all those men made her think differently, and Liza was still a knockout at her age. They went on with their adulterous ways for years before things began to unravel.

Liza was concerned about a woman Berlin was so enamored by. She began to follow Berlin the nights she knew he was staying out with her. She never saw him with a woman. Puzzled by her findings, she evaluated what was before her. She thought, maybe it was always Jean and Berlin she saw together, and they were designing something without her. That made her angry even more so. They agreed to never do that. Their designs would be between themselves and their company. She wanted to confront him, but didn't know how to approach him about it.

She paced the floor waiting for him to return home. He did, three hours later. Liza called him from the library. Walking into the library with a smile on his face, he spoke, "Hello, Liza dear."

He kissed her on the cheek. Returning the kiss, she said. "Hello dear. I asked you here because something isn't right. You've been different. I think it's because you and Jean are designing behind my back and not giving me my share."

Berlin laughed, "Darling, is that what you think? No, that isn't true. I would never do you that way, Liza. We have been business partners for too long for that." Liza, laughing, with her head held down, spoke, "Excuse me, that was utter foolishness, I apologize." "You're forgiven." Berlin leaned toward Liza and kissed her on the lips ever so gently. Liza melted like a Popsicle on a hot summer day.

Closing the library door, Berlin took Liza right then and there. They stripped each other's clothes off and made hot passionate love for hours. Liza was in heaven; however, she knew he was cheating, but with whom? After they finished, they showered and ate dinner. Berlin left the house at twelve midnight. He told Liza he had a fashion show to go to with Jean. When he left, Liza poured herself a glass of wine and sat there thinking about her mother, Estrada. Estrada had been in prison for twenty years now for killing Liza's father and grandfather for what they did to her. It all happened on a hot summer day, twenty years ago.

Estrada decided to finally take care of that problem. She went to Clyde's house and shot him in the head six times. No one noticed him for hours because she had a silencer. Leaving there, she headed home and waited for Lance. Pulling up in the driveway, Lance got out of the car and slammed the car door shut. Walking to the door with keys in hand, he unlocked the door. He walked to the kitchen and placed his briefcase on the counter. He noticed the T.V. was extremely loud, so he walked into the living room. As he reached the center of the room, Estrada jumped out behind him with gun in hand. She spoke, "You thought this was over. I told you that you would pay. I just knocked off good old Clyde, your dad. Now it's your turn." He turned, facing her with fear in his eyes. She pulled the trigger. She unloaded, reloaded and unloaded once more. Turning off the T.V., she called the police. They arrested her, and she was charged with two counts of first degree murder. They couldn't prove it was premeditated because the defense attorney, Leman Brooks, proved reasonable doubt, so they sentenced her to second degree murder. Estrada was sentenced to seventy years in prison. She had served twenty years so far. She had fifty years to go. She killed them both three months after Liza and her family were here to visit. That was the last time Estrada was on the street.

Liza was glad her mom took care of that, but she wished her mom didn't have to sit in prison for it. She sat back and poured herself another glass of wine. She didn't feel like seeing her men today, so she relaxed at home.

Berlin was gone a week. He was in a city twelve hours outside of Paris doing a fashion show with Jean. They were all due to go on tour with the new Hamgorium gear clothing line in a month. Liza was just taking it easy until then. She thought about Berlin some more. She knew he was seeing someone; she wasn't sure whom. She looked in the mirror and spoke to herself. "Look at me! Who can compete with all this lusciousness? Nobody can, so if he is cheating, he's a damn fool." Walking away from the mirror, she headed to her bedroom.

CHAPTER SIX

The down low

Berlin and Jean were back from their fashion tour. Liza was excited about the press they received. She was ready for their three month tour. Liza was on her way to work. Berlin stayed home to rest, and Jean went to the shop. He worked with Liza for an hour; then he clocked out and left. Liza wasn't leaving for another three hours. She worked her fingers to the bone that day. She was disappointed because Berlin was gone when she got home. He wouldn't answer her calls.

Angry, she slammed the phone down and fixed herself a drink. She was determined to know who this mystery lady was that had Berlin in the palm of her hands. She decided to call Bronze over; she knew his wife was at work and that he could come over. He was there in no time. Stripping off each other's clothes, they went at it. An hour had gone by when they exploded together. Afterwards, Liza lit up a cigarette, breathing hard. Bronze got dressed and left. Liza made arrangements to see him again in three days. She knew Berlin would be off with Little Miss Slut. Berlin stayed out all night and didn't return home until the next day. They saw each other at work and said not a word to one another.

Berlin, Liza, Jean, and several of the staff were leaving for New York in two weeks. Liza reserved dinner at an exclusive restaurant for three hours for her and the family. She set it up for that night. She called the children and told them about it. Their husbands and children were coming. Before leaving the office, she told Berlin about the family dinner tonight.

Liza went home and picked out one of her gowns she just designed. When folks heard they were dining there, everybody that could afford to eat there came. Everyone was having a good time, until Berlin tried to leave early. Liza, in a fury, yelled. "Where are you going? Off to see your mistress, that witch? You're having dinner with your family. That cunt can wait. Every time she calls, you jump up and run. It's like you're her puppet." Berlin shot back. "Shut up, Liza! This is why we have problems now. You're always talking to me recklessly. You have no respect for me. You don't have any idea. Do you want to know who my mistress is? I've been living with him now for six months. That's why I'm never home. I will be home to get the rest of my things, and I'm filing for a divorce. It's over, Liza."

"It's over, but you can't tell me who he is? And what do you mean it is a he?"

Everyone was speechless. Lana tried to comfort her mother, but there was no consoling Liza. She was hysterical. Berlin left and so did Liza. The meals were already paid for. The Hamgorium girls ran out behind their parents with their own families in tow. They all went to Liza's house.

They arrived just as Liza did. She was so far gone it was sad. Just as she walked in the house, the phone rang. It was Berlin. With a mean tone to his voice, he spoke. "You can keep the house and we can still be business partners. One more thing, you better go and get checked for HIV because Jean has it, and I was diagnosed three months ago."

Liza yelled. "You nasty bastard, you had unprotected sex with me a week ago, and you have HIV? Berlin, I am going to kill you if I have HIV. You can tell Jean he's fired. As a matter of fact, I'll tell him myself."

She hung up the phone and immediately called her physician. She explained her dilemma, and he came right over to draw blood. The girls were mad at their dad. They couldn't believe he had HIV and their mom might have it. They didn't know what to say, and neither did Liza.

After awhile they left and headed for home. Liza called her sister, Keanu and told her of the mess. Keanu was so worried about Liza, she offered to fly there and be with her. Liza assured her she was fine, that she could handle it, and hung up.

Liza drank herself into a stupor and was falling all over the floor. She was nervous about the test. Her doctor told her he could get STAT results. He said he would call within a three hour time span. It was three hours exactly, and the phone rang. Her results were negative. But he told her he wanted to check her again in three months because that disease can lay dormant for years before it shows up. She was afraid but relieved. She called her daughters and told them of the good news. They were glad to hear that she was negative. She didn't tell them the other part. She let them have their peace of mind. Liza couldn't believe her husband was on the down low, a bi-sexual man. She tried to shake the thought, but she couldn't.

CHAPTER SEVEN

The knock offs

Liza got her way. Jean was fired, but he and Berlin were still in a relationship. Business was still booming for Liza and Berlin. They were training the girls on how to take over as it was becoming too much for them. Two of the girls worked there. London was an executive president as well as a designer, and Latasha was a designer and a seamstress. They knew the business well and had been working there since they were out of high school.

Liza was on medication now. She had become mentally unstable after Berlin broke her heart. She was on sleeping pills, anxiety pills, nerve pills, and antidepressants. She tried coping with her issue, but that didn't stop her from seeing her five men.

Latasha began to notice a change in her husband, Michael. He was working late hours often. She knew they needed the money, but she was concerned. She thought no more of it.

Liza was getting angry because each one of her men was married. They always had to leave and go home to their wives, and she was growing tired of that. She began to plot ways to kill their wives, one by one. She wanted the men all to herself.

Liza went in for her second blood test; it was negative. She was glad. She had to get tested two more times to be safe. Six months had gone by, and she was still having an affair with all five of her men. She wasn't stopping either.

It was now December. Liza was due for her last blood draw. She waited in the doctor's office with a smile on her face. Her doctor came out. The results were positive, Liza had HIV. The doctor had to pick her up off the floor. She was yelling in agony. The doctor ordered the nurse to take her in a room. Once they were there, Liza was given a drink of water and a prescription to control the HIV virus. Liza decided not to tell anyone, not even her own children.
She really began to plot the murders now because she was angry at the world.

Liza made it through the winter, still looking fabulous. It was summer time. Liza was glad to still be alive, and Berlin was looking ill. Liza stayed home this day, drinking heavily. Night fall came, and she was still drinking. It was now three in the morning. Liza took a three mile drive to the lavish neighborhood where Michael stayed. She knew his house; she had been there before. Clipping the brake line on his wife's car, she slipped back into her car and headed home.

Once she was home, she pulled off her clothes and climbed into her bed. When she awakened, it was 9:00 a.m. She decided not to work. Instead, she went shopping. Just as she was putting her things in the car, her phone rang. It was Leann, crying and screaming at the top of her lungs, saying, "It's Latasha, Mom. She was in a car accident on the freeway, and she's gone. Mom, did you hear me? Latasha is dead! Meet us at the hospital in downtown Paris."

Liza jumped in her car and headed to the hospital. When she got there, Michael and everybody else was there. Berlin was there, too. All you could hear was crying and screaming. Everyone left and headed to Latasha's house.

Michael put the kids to bed, and they all talked. No one knew what happened. All they knew was that she crashed. The police confiscated the car to do an investigation. Liza was standing there sobbing, knowing darn well she killed her own daughter. A week went by. Latasha's funeral was over. Now Liza was preparing to sue the car company on behalf of Latasha's family. The police thought the brake line failed. Liza was no dummy. She snipped it where it looked like it snapped instead. The lawsuit took three years before they were awarded a twenty million dollar lawsuit. Eight million was given to Berlin and Liza because it was their daughter. Michael and the children were given twelve million. No one was the wiser. Now Liza had Michael all to herself.

Two years after Latasha's death, everyone was healing and moving on. That year Liza and Berlin made it; they were named the richest people in the world. They were worth billions. Liza announced another family dinner to celebrate. She let Lahti pick the restaurant this time. It was set for the next night. Jean was coming this time, and Liza was happy about it. Liza dressed up fabulously, ready to go. Her chauffeur took her to the restaurant. With her concoction in her purse, she was ready. She made a grand entrance. The family was there waiting for her. No one could tell that she and Michael, Latasha's widow, were a pair. Everyone ordered their food and hit the dance floor. Liza stayed behind. She knew where everyone was sitting.

Once the food arrived, she quickly dropped liquid into Jean and Latasha's children's food and drinks. When the song was over, everyone came to the table and began to eat. They all sat and talked for awhile before leaving. It was twelve midnight. The kids were tired, so they left. Liza kissed all ten of her grandchildren before leaving.

Michael put the children to bed when he got home. They had plans to go to the zoo the next day, and they were excited. The alarm went off eight in the morning. Michael went to the kitchen to start the coffee pot. Stretching and yawning, he headed to Collin's room. Knocking on the door, there was no response. He entered, speaking loudly. "Wake up! Let's have breakfast!" No response. He walked over to the bed, pulling the covers back. Michael screamed. Collin was blue in the face. He was dead. Michael ran to the phone and called the police. With the phone in hand, he raced to his daughter Doreen's room. He was afraid; he called her name and no response. He pulled her covers back. She was blue and dead, too. Michael ran out of the house screaming. "My children are dead! My children are dead! Somebody help me please!"

Neighbors came from everywhere. Michael lost his mind; he was not functional at all. He rode in the ambulance with his children. He had a neighbor call Lana.

The news of the children's death spread fast. Berlin had three broken hearts because his lover Jean and his grandchildren were gone. Liza could have won an academy award; she mourned like she really meant it. Michael sued the restaurant because arsenic was found in the kid's system during the autopsy. The restaurant was fined thousands of dollars, and Michael received ten million dollars in his lawsuit. Liza decided to hire Leann to take the place of Latasha.

Two years had gone by since the kids' death. Liza was brewing an idea to knock off her other four daughters and their two kids. She had the perfect idea, for Leann. Liza's friend, Kathy, needed help at her store, so she offered up Leann to help, and Leann accepted the idea. Liza knew Leann would work alone Saturday night. On Friday night Liza stopped by Leann's job to see how it was working out. Before leaving, she went to the restroom, so they thought. She detoured to the basement, placing a bomb in the furnace. Liza had it set to detonate in twenty four hours. Heading back upstairs to the restroom, Liza walked in, flushed the toilet, and left, kissing Leann on the cheek and exiting the door calmly. Liza woke up the next morning in good spirits. She knew Leann was done for today. She got dressed for work, looking in the mirror. Liza smiled, saying out loud. "Four down, eight to go."

It was now nine in the evening. Kathy's store was full, and Leann was busy. Suddenly, boom! The bomb had detonated. Leann and all the customers were blown up in the store. The police were called, and the store owner across the street called Kathy, screaming.

"Kathy, your store just blew up. Leann and all those customers were in there. Girl, you better get here quick."

"Ok Donna, I'm coming." Kathy was crying, because that was her livelihood up in flames. When Kathy got there and saw it, she screamed in horror. She quickly dialed Liza and told her what happened. Liza played dumb. When Liza pulled up, she yelled at Kathy. "I'm suing your black behind. Your building was faulty, and you had my baby up in there." With tears rolling down her face, she called Berlin and the rest of the family. London was too far gone. She couldn't believe the death angel that loomed over her family, and for what? The police did their investigation and found the explosive, but there wasn't a print on it. Liza still won her lawsuit because they believed Kathy had problems with someone that caused it. She was held responsible in civil court. Liza was paid once again for a bogus suit that she caused.

There were only three of the Hamgorium girls left with their children. Leann's kids were still alive so far. Liza was getting older, but she was still beautiful. She was still carrying on her affairs with her daughter's husband Philip. During that time he was still puzzled by Leann's death.

The kids were all due back in school; they had been out for summer vacation. Liza decided to do a family trip to an amusement park. The kids were excited; they needed some fun after all they had been through. The oldest grandchildren were fifteen and sixteen. They were London and Merck's kids. She knew killing them would be difficult, because they were older. They were having a ball at the amusement park. Liza rode some rides with the kids, as did Merck and Philip. As they walked through the amusement park, they spotted a roller coaster. Liza suggested they ride it. Leann and Philip's two kids, Dana and Jason, rode, as did London and Merck's son, Devon. They had made it to the front of the line; it was their turn to ride. The roller coaster came to a halt and let the passengers off. They all got on and waited for the bar to close and lock. Liza had her hand on the unlock button for her grandson, Devon. She kept her hand on that switch until the bar closed and locked. Devon's didn't lock, but Liza's did. The roller coaster took off. Down they went at one hundred miles per hour. They got to the upside down loop, and Devon fell from the roller coaster. Everyone that was watching screamed in horror. They couldn't stop the ride in mid air; so it kept going. It seemed like forever. Someone screamed, "Oh my God, somebody's child fell from the roller coaster in mid air! He's dead." Every parent that had a child on the ride pushed their way up to the front to see if it was their kid. When London made it to the front, she screamed, "Oh! God, it's my baby." She tried climbing over the railing and across the roller coaster tracks to hold her baby, but security stopped her. London passed out. Merck was at a game with Lana, Bronze, Dana, and Jason, so he didn't know his son was dead.

The roller coaster stopped. Liza was sitting there, balling. The EMS had to come for her and London, too. Lana and the rest of the family had come back to the roller coaster, and they noticed all the mayhem. A loud voice came over the loud speaker, saying, "Will the Hamgorium family please report to the front of the roller coaster?" Their hearts were pounding. They grabbed all the kids and made their way to the front of the line. They saw Liza and London on a stretcher. They saw Leann's two children and grabbed them. Lana saw a body under a white sheet and yelled. "Who is that under the sheet?" They wouldn't say. Lana angrily yelled again. "I'm going to ask one more time. Who is that under that sheet?" London, awakening after passing out, yelled, "It's Devon, Lana!" Merck lost it. "London, he yelled. What the hell, happened? No, not this again!" Liza, still playing the victim, was the cold- hearted killer.

London sued the amusement park. She and her husband received a one hundred million dollar settlement for Devon's death. The amusement park closed that ride indefinitely. They built a brand new one.

A year after receiving the settlement, London had a nervous breakdown and was placed in a hospital. The nurse gave London something to help her sleep twenty minutes before Liza arrived. Once she was asleep, Liza pulled a needle out of her purse. It was filled with insulin. Slowly, London slipped into a coma. Liza was hoping she didn't make it. London remained in her coma for a month. When she woke up, all she remembered was the nurse giving her some medicine to help her sleep, she didn't remember talking to her mom.

The hospital started an investigation on the nurse that gave her the injection. They found no reason for the coma, but stress. London didn't want to sue because it would have been hard to prove the hospital was negligent. She was glad to be alive. London was released from the hospital three weeks after her coma. All her tests came back normal; she was doing fine.

Two months later, Lana was in the hospital. She was struck with pneumonia. She was weak and very ill. She kept a fever of one hundred and three. She slept all the time. The doctors thought she was going to die. Liza was there to visit her every day. The hospital thought she was a good mother. The nurse came in and gave Lana an injection. Liza calmly asked,

"What is that you are giving her?"

"Fentanyl, it will help her sleep."

On the way out, Liza saw a bottle of fentanyl on the nurse's cart and took it.

Driving home, she devised a plan. Once she arrived, she poured a glass of wine and slammed it. She poured another and slammed that one, too. That knocked the edge off. Liza poured another and headed to her sun room. There she pulled out the medication she had stolen and a syringe. She filled the syringe with the fentanyl. She wanted to know how it felt; so she injected herself with a small dose of it. After that, she replaced the small dose and wrapped it in a handkerchief and placed it in her purse.

Liza fell asleep in the sunroom. She awakened at 10:00 a.m. the next day. She showered, got dressed and headed down to see Lana. When she got there, Lana was worse. The doctor came in and told Liza that Lana was suffering from a staph infection in her lungs. Liza began to drop those fake tears, but on the inside she was glad. Now she could proceed with her plan. Liza walked in the room; everyone was there. Berlin spoke. "Liza, can we talk?"

"Sure."

"My dad passed away last night. I haven't told the girl's yet. I'm trying to wait for Lana to pull through. I'll be leaving tonight, but if anything happens to Lana, call me. I'll be back here right away."

Liza just nodded her head, saying nothing. She turned and headed back to Lana's room. Kissing her forehead, she sat next to her. While talking to everybody, she rubbed Lana on the hand. Liza walked down and grabbed a cup of coffee and returned back to Lana's room. Liza was cool; she sat there reading her book and watching television. Again she began to talk to Lana. The nurse walked in and was glad to see that. The nurse spoke, "That is so wonderful, asking her if she wants to watch T.V. She can hear we just got her on fentanyl. She was in a lot of pain when she came in here."

The nurse checked her vitals and gave her a dose of fentanyl. Smiling at Liza, the nurse exited the room. Liza reached into her purse and grabbed her syringe filled with the medication the nurse just gave Lana. Liza injected Lana with every drop in the same port the nurse injected into, quickly putting it back in her purse. Lana's machines began to beep. Liza ran out screaming. "Nurse, help me!"

Nurses and doctors came from everywhere with crash carts, closing the door behind them. They quickly began to work on Lana. Ten minutes later, the doctor came out and told Liza, "I'm sorry Mrs.

Hamgorium, but she didn't make it." Liza fell to the floor screaming. She was beside herself.

Pulling herself together, she called Berlin. This was horrible - first his father, now his daughter. After she called him, she called Lahti. It traveled to the others. They all rushed back to the hospital. It was a sad occasion. London was in a daze; she couldn't believe this was happening. She left with her husband and daughter. Once they were home, Merck had to help her into the house. She screamed in agonizing pain. All she kept saying was "Another, sister, another death, I can't believe it." Merck held her and cried. He has never seen anything like this before. This was unheard of, all these deaths. Berlin called his mother, crying while he was driving. Asti was so affected, she suffered a heart attack that night in her sleep. This was all too much for her.

Berlin went to sleep drunk around three in the morning. Suddenly his phone rang. He answered, "Hello." A strong husky voice spoke. "Is this Berlin Hamgorium?"

"Who is this?"

"My name is detective Marlow; I'm calling you from Florida." Sitting up alongside his bed, shaking off the drunkenness and lighting a cigarette, he spoke, "Yes, this is Berlin Hamgorium."

"I'm sorry to tell you this, but the housekeeper found your mother dead in bed this morning."

"No! No! No! Come on man, not my mother, too. Oh, God!" He was in shock. He couldn't bring himself to tell the rest of the family; they just lost Lana hours ago. He called Lahti and told her about the death of her grandma. Now they had to bury three instead of two.

Berlin flew to Florida and had his parents shipped to Paris, and they had Lana, Asti, and Kumar's funeral together. After the funerals, London and her family decided to leave Paris. She couldn't take it anymore. Something told her not to tell anyone about her plans, and she didn't. They decided to move to Tennessee. They found a home, and a month later they moved. Once they were settled, she called Lahti and told her where they had moved. Lahti was angry, but still understood why she moved away. When Liza found out, she was infuriated. Now London was really untouchable.

Liza was sixty two years old now. Her HIV problem was beginning to show. She was losing weight, and her hair was falling out. A year had gone by since Lana died. Once again, Liza received a tidy sum for her death, too. The nurse was fired. They had found a high dose of the same drug the nurse gave. So they figured the nurse did it. No one was the wiser.

Back in Tennessee, London, Merck, and her daughter were doing fine. London was thinking of all that happened. The Holy Spirit began to open her mind.

London began to do her own investigation. She got out the newspaper article on Latasha's car crash and Leann's accident. There was something diabolical, about each death. She thought about how Latasha and her children died. She wondered if someone poisoned those children on purpose, but who? Growing tired, she headed to bed with notes in hand.

It's now a year later, December 2009. Lahti and Bronze were having another baby. That would make baby number three. It was a Friday afternoon. Liza volunteered to come over and help Lahti out around the house. Bronze was gone to work, and the children were in school. They were having a good time laughing and talking. They had cleaned the entire house and were starting the laundry. Lahti loved exercising, so she grabbed the laundry basket and headed downstairs. As soon as she opened the basement door, Liza pushed Lahti down the stairs. She hit the bottom, Liza stood there looking at her before she called for help. The ambulance came quickly. Once they reached Lahti, she was dead. She died from a broken neck. The baby didn't make it either, Lahti was five months pregnant.

London didn't attend the funeral; she couldn't handle burying her only sister that was left. All her nieces and nephews were grown and in college. Now Liza had them all to herself: Philip, Bronze, John, and Michael. As for Merck, she was working on him being a widower, too. She still wanted Merck. Liza sat up all night thinking about how to get him and kill London. She picked up the phone and called London. "Hello, replied London."

"It's your mom, how are you London?"

"I'm fine Mom, and how are you?"

"I was wondering when I will get a visit."

"It has been awhile, hasn't it?"

"It sure has, I just miss you, that's all."

"How about in two weeks?"

"Wonderful, see you then."

Happier than a kid in a candy store, she had London's death planned, too. Liza was ready. She patiently waited for London to come and visit. While waiting, she continued her affairs with all her son-in-laws. London was due to see her mother in a week. She continued to think about all the deaths. She knew for a fact her mother was there when Lana and Lahti were accidentally killed, so the police said. London went back through her articles. Hours had passed. It was 5:00 p.m. Bible study started at six, she knew she had time to look over more articles before leaving.

Chapter eight

Cold busted by

Back in Paris, Berlin was close to death. He was told he had three years to live. His HIV had developed into full blown AIDS. It was time for London to go home. Her husband, Merck, had left home a week prior. He told London he had a business trip in Detroit and that he would be back in two weeks. London never said where she was going. If Merck knew what she was up to, he would have stopped her from going. London was going to investigate all the deaths in her family.

When London arrived in Paris, Liza had her driver pick her up from the airport. When she arrived at Liza's house, she was calm. Liza saw her pulling up and ran to meet her outside. Liza greeted her with a hug and a kiss. Walking inside, Liza was telling her about the reservations for dinner.

London knew what she meant; she couldn't believe her mother was still in touch with her sisters' husbands. She made a mental note of that. London stayed in touch with her nieces and nephews. She reserved a room two miles from the home she grew up in, the one Liza still lives in, but she stayed, and talked, and laughed with her mother for awhile.

Noticing the time, she headed to her hotel to get ready for dinner. Liza even invited Berlin to dinner. They all had a wonderful time at dinner. London was glad to see Michael, Philip, Bronze, and John. She hadn't seen them since they moved away.

London decided to head back to Tennessee that night, so she decided to go back and see Liza. She didn't call because she had a key to let herself in. She called her dad, Berlin, and asked him to meet her there because she was going back home. He was more than happy to meet her there. London arrived first. Letting herself in, she heard music blaring from upstairs. It was opera music; Liza loved it. London headed up to her mother's room. The bedroom door was closed. London, slowly pushing the door open, had the shock of her life. Bronze, Michael, Philip, John, and Merck were in bed with Liza. They were all naked engaging in wild sex. London turned and ran, puking all over the place as she was leaving. She couldn't believe what she saw. Her mother was sleeping with all her sister's husbands and hers, too. London was sick. Just then, Berlin arrived at the home as London was leaving. He could tell something was wrong with his daughter. Reaching for her, he asked, "What's wrong, London?" Pointing upstairs, Berlin took off upstairs, afraid of what might be. Running into the bedroom, he, too, was shocked by what he saw. They all stopped and threw on robes. Liza turned off the stereo and ran downstairs, and her son-in-laws followed. Berlin yelled, "What is wrong with you, Liza? What are you doing? Everyone sit!" Liza, about to say something, was interrupted by Berlin. He yelled once more, "Shut up! Liza. London, baby, this is all going to hurt, so I hope you came here in a strong forgiving mood." He paused. "First, I want to say that your mother and I divorced because I was in a relationship with Jean."

"Jean? Daddy please, you're not talking about Uncle Jean, the one that worked for you and mama?"

"Yes, Uncle Jean."

"You mean to tell me that you're a homosexual?"

"Bisexual, London."

"It's all the same to me, Daddy."

"There's more. Bronze and I have been seeing each other for five years now." Liza, angered, jumped out of her seat. She socked Bronze in the face. In the background you could hear London yelling, "Lord, No! No Lord, this can't be happening."

Liza yelled, "You and Berlin have been seeing each other, too?" Berlin spoke again saying, "That's not all."

"There's more Daddy? How much betrayal is left?"

"London, I have AIDS." Gasping for air, she sat down. At that moment, Liza, angrier than before, spoke, "Now I will have full blown AIDS. London, he gave me HIV, too; I just never told anyone." They all began to fight. Fists were flying everywhere, and everybody was hitting each other. It went on for what seemed like forever. When it was all over, there was blood everywhere. London, after fixing her clothes and hair, spoke calmly, "I never want to see any of you again, and as for you Merck, get your hind parts back to Tennessee right now, and get your crap out of my house. We are done." Walking towards the door, she stopped and turned, facing them. "You nasty bastards better hope I don't have AIDS, cause if I do .... "

Looking at her mother, London walked up to her and stood in her face, giving her a dirty look, saying, "By the way Mom, I'm on to you. You better hope I don't find out the truth about my sisters, because if I do, you're going to the slammer for life." She turned and grimly walked away. Berlin yelled, "What is she talking about, Liza?"

Looking at them all, she spoke, "Shut up and get out, all of you." She shoved them out the door and slammed it behind them. They all left.

She had to figure out a way to kill London because she was too close to the truth. London headed to the airport to go home. She knew she was right about her mother, but she had to prove it. Merck never came to retrieve his clothes. He stayed in Paris with Liza.

Two weeks had gone by and Liza had a final curtain call. It was eleven o'clock at night. Merck was sleeping in the recliner chair. Liza, with a loaded gun and a silencer attached to it, shot Merck in the head. He died instantly. She made her way to John's house. Ringing his doorbell, John peeped out the door to see Liza. Letting her in, asking no questions, they kissed passionately. They made their way to his home office, which was their favorite place to have sex when she came over. Closing the door behind them, they stripped off their clothes and headed for the sofa. Stroking her like always, Liza enjoyed it. Once they were done, Liza lit a cigarette. Reaching in her purse, she pulled out her gun. John couldn't say a word; Liza unloaded on him, too. She was planning to go down the line until all her son-in-law lovers were dead. Berlin was going to be her last stop. He was a bonus for her, because he started it all.

The 3:30 p.m. school bell rang, and Jessica and Martin hopped into the car and headed home after stopping at the store, they arrived home thirty minutes later than their usual time. Pulling into the garage, they got of the car grabbing their book bags and laughing at their teacher, Mr. Simpler, because he tripped and fell in class today. Walking in the house, Jessica yelled, "Dad, we're home." They heard nothing. They found their dad dead on the floor in his office, with his head blown into pieces. They ran out of the house. Jessica called the police from her cell phone and Martin called his aunts. Everyone rushed to the scene.

Liza thought about everything Berlin did to her. She thought about his staying away for days, his leaving late at night. She pulled up to her house, went inside and poured a glass of wine. With glass in hand, she headed for the bathroom. She decided to shower and to call Philip to see if he wanted to come over. He told her he would be over in an hour. Liza knew that she had plenty of time to shower and prepare for his murder. She poured another glass. After showering, she headed for the bedroom. Sitting at the vanity in her room, she began to paint her nails and think about all the daughters she had murdered and the ones she hadn't.

While drying her nails, she began to laugh. She knew everything was going according to her wicked plan. She brushed her hair, rolled it up to a bun, and pinned it in place. She dabbed on her perfume and picked the earrings and necklace she would wear. She wore an evening gown. Liza still hadn't lost her beauty or knockout of a body at her age. The doorbell rang; she knew it was Philip. With a cigarette and her clutch bag in hand, she walked downstairs. Philip stepped inside and asked, "Where are we going?" Smiling, Liza said, "Out on the town, honey." She threw him the keys and headed to the car. Liza had the night planned. They were headed to a town twelve hours from Paris. They were going out to dinner, dancing, karaoke, and to a cabin that no one knew about, except for Liza. They stopped at Machete restaurant. The food was expensive, delicious, and worth every dollar. There was a dance club two miles from the restaurant, so they headed there afterwards. The club was jumping. When they walked inside, a woman at the door stamped their hand and gave them a glow – in – the - dark necklace. Dancing through the crowd, they finally made it to Liza's table and waited for a waitress to arrive. They ordered their drinks and headed to the dance floor. Dancing the night away, they had a ball. They knew it was late, but they didn't care, they were having fun. Upon leaving the dance club, they spotted a casino across the street and decided to gamble for a bit. Drinking and having a blast with a pocket full of winnings, they called it a night and headed to Liza's cabin. On the way there Philip thanked Liza for the night out.

Arriving at the cabin, Philip couldn't believe how well maintained and high tech it was. Everything was voice activated. A bottle of wine was in an ice bucket on the table, and Liza went to the kitchen to grab some glasses. Philip loosened his tie and poured the wine. He turned on the T.V. and found a game of golf. Liza slipped into something more comfortable and returned with a teddy and robe on. Sipping on her wine, she grabbed some snacks from the kitchen and sat next to Philip on the sofa. They ate snacks and watched golf, until it ended.

They made their way to the bedroom. Philip, in a drunken stupor, finished undressing. He got in bed and turned on the T.V. Liza, stripped down to nothing, climbed on top of him and kissed him from head to toe. Pulling out a pair of handcuffs, Philip smiled. Liza handcuffed him to the bedpost. With ice pick in hand, she licked Philip from his stomach to his mouth, and then she stabbed him in one ear, then in the other. Screaming in pain, he knew death was near. Liza reached for her purse. She pulled out a syringe. It was a concoction of battery acid and bleach. Squirming and trying to get out of the cuffs, Philip felt the injection. Immediately his face turned red, and he began to sweat and convulse. Liza got dressed and headed for the closet, where she kept an accelerant. Throwing on a pair of gloves, she began to douse the bedroom and the bed. She made her way down the hallway, the kitchen, and the living room. She opened the front door, stepped on the porch, and made sure she dropped some at the entrance to set the cabin on fire. With lighter in hand, she lit a napkin and dropped it in the doorway. Quickly, she made her way to the car and left, looking at the flames from her rearview mirror. She knew this was a perfect plan. She knew she wouldn't get caught because no one knew they were up there, and the cabin wasn't registered to Liza.

Driving home, she was relaxed with no remorse for what she had done. It was 10:00 a.m. when Liza arrived home. Tired from her night, she showered and went to bed. She turned on the T.V. and began to think of how she could get rid of Leann and Philip's children, but her focus right now was London, because she still had her husband, Merck, and Liza felt Merck was her's.

The next morning Liza awakened with a plan in mind to finish what she started. Bronze was on her list tonight. Liza spent all day drinking. She was preparing for her trip to Tennessee to kill London because she knew London was on her trail. Liza had gotten away with all the other murders and she felt invincible. Bronze was at work and Liza knew that. She waited until dusk to call him. She told him she wanted to see him, and he agreed. She went to his house and waited. She decided to make a romantic dinner. She set the table with candles, a beautiful table cloth, and some rose petals. She dimmed the lights to set the mood and poured herself a glass of wine. Once he arrived, they kissed passionately. Liza looked into his eyes and said,

"I missed you so much, Bronze." Shocked that she still wanted him, he asked, "You're not angry about Berlin and me? After our secret was let out, I broke it off. I wanted you more than him." With a smile on her face, she didn't respond. They talked about their future together, and even what they were going to do for the rest of the night. They were ready to make love. They took off their clothes and headed to the basement. Liza wanted to have sex down there because there was a pole that she could hang Bronze from. With handcuffs in hand, she whispered, "I've got a surprise for you, and you're going to love it." After she handcuffed him to the ceiling, she tied his feet to two beams that protruded from the floor. With his legs and arms spread apart, he knew he was going to have crazy sex tonight. Liza turned on some music and began to dance for Bronze. Getting hard, he smiled saying, "Yea baby, shake that ass!" As she stroked his shaft with her mouth, he began to moan. She knew it was time to strike. Pulling a knife from a tissue box, she sliced his penis completely off and put it in his mouth to muffle his screams. He fought to get loose, but to no avail. Liza grabbed a broom, and with a smile on her face, she said, "This is bigger and longer than Berlin! You're going to love this." Angry, she shoved the broomstick up his ass with no lubrication. Tightening his anal passage, she shoved it further. Over half of it was in there. He was in so much pain, he fainted. Liza filled a bucket with cold water to wake him up. He spit his penis out of his mouth. Liza waited to see if he would talk. He was in so much pain, he couldn't. She tried forcing his penis back in his mouth, but he wouldn't open it. She sliced him across his stomach, and he screamed in pain. She quickly shoved it down his throat. He began to choke on it. Turning off the music, she left and went up stairs. She cleaned herself, got dressed and left. She knew he would die. She wanted him to suffer.

It was 11:00 p.m. She was on her way to Berlin. She decided to just show up and not call him. After arriving, she rang the doorbell. He answered, surprised that Liza came to see him. Once inside, he offered her a drink and asked, "What have I done to deserve a visit from you?" Liza cleared her throat and said, "Berlin, I know you are very ill and you are going to die. I just want us to patch things up before you do. I don't want you to leave this earth with us mad at each other." Surprised by her willingness to forgive him, he began to smile. He raised his glass and said, "A toast to better days." Raising her glass, she said, "To better days and better times." Finishing off their drinks, Liza grabbed her purse and gave Berlin a hug saying, "Got to go, I will see you soon." As she headed toward the door, she said, "Oh, one more thing." With her back to him she reached in her purse, then quickly turned to face him. He didn't have a chance to react; she pulled the trigger and unloaded on him. She closed the door behind her and left. Her job was done in Paris. Now she was headed to Tennessee to find London.

That morning, London got out of bed and called the detectives that handled each of her sister's cases. She told them what she thought and what she believed happened. They were shocked to hear that her mother could be responsible for her own daughters' and grandchildren's death.

The detectives went back and talked to the man at the amusement park that was running the roller coaster that day. He told the detectives that he remembered double - checking his bar, and it was locked. He also told them about the switch on the lower right side to unlock, that you had to know how to unlock it, once it was locked. He showed the detectives where it was. He told them that Liza and that boy were seated together. The detectives left and headed over to the store to talk to some of the customers that were questioned about the explosion at the store. There was a woman that was never questioned. They spoke to her. Detective Logo asked the questions while the other detective wrote down the answers. Logo began to talk. "Tell me what you know, Ms. Jones."

"Well, I was coming out of the bathroom. I had just finished shopping. There was a woman coming up the stairs from the basement. That woman was Liza Hamgorium, the famous designer. Her daughter was helping out in the store. Poor girl, she was killed. I had just loaded my bags in the car when all of a sudden, Boom! The store was gone."

"Did you see Liza leave?"

"Yes, I did. She was just getting to her car when the store blew up."

"Thanks, Ms. Jones."

Leaving with their new found information, they headed back to their office. They looked at the brake line on Latasha's car that they had in evidence. Detective Logo noticed the smooth break. He thought, if this broke, then it should be rough and jagged. He was angered by the way the other detective handled this. Logo inherited this case six months ago, reopened it, and followed up on it. He just got the break he needed to crack this case.

London was warned by the Holy Spirit that her mother was coming for her, and she knew to obey the voice of GOD. So she checked herself into a hotel suite, in case she located her house. Once she was settled in her suite, she called the detectives in Paris and the police in her home town in Tennessee. The police in Tennessee thought she was crazy, but the police in Paris were put on alert. The Paris police called London back and let her know she was being guarded, and they contacted the Tennessee police department to let them know what was going on.

The police in Paris had enough information to ask for a search warrant. They obtained one immediately. They went right to Liza's house and searched. They found arsenic, fentanyl, the material to make the bomb, and the gloves she wore. They were ready to arrest Liza, but they couldn't find her. They began to look for her in Tennessee, too. Liza's lovers all died without knowing they had HIV. She was still on the stroll looking for London.

Relaxing at the hotel, London had a doctor come and draw her blood. The first test was negative.

Relieved, she waited for the police to call. She wanted her mother to pay for what she done.

Hours had gone by, and Liza was nowhere in sight. After rigorous searching, Liza finally found out where London lived. Pulling up to her house, she got out of the car with her gun drawn. She got on the porch to ring the door bell and heard, "Freeze! Liza Hamgorium, you are under arrest. You have the right to remain silent. Anything you say can and will be used against you in a court of law. You have the right to an attorney. If you can't afford one, one will be appointed for you. You do understand what I've just told you." Dropping her gun, she turned to them saying. "So be it, I don't have long anyway. I have AIDS." Showing no sympathy for her, they slapped the cuffs on her, hauling her lying, manipulative, chocolate behind to jail. Liza knew it was all over. She was going to prison. She was getting letters, not numbers.

Once she was in the interrogation room, she coldly admitted to the murders of her daughters. She even told them to send the coroner to Berlin, Philip, Michael, Bronze, and John's, and back to her house. Detective Keep spoke, "Your house, for what?" She laughed. "Merck is at my house. Go upstairs in my room, you will see a tall bookshelf. The bookshelf is from ceiling to floor. Pull out the tenth book from the left on the fourth shelf. The shelf will swing open inward. He's in there, dead." They called the police in Paris and told them what Liza just revealed. They checked it out, and they all were dead in their homes. London heard the story on the news. She was angry and burst into tears. It was confirmed that her mother was cold-hearted and a murderer. Her mother had just about wiped out the entire family. There was barely any immediate family left, now that Liza had murdered everyone, except for London, her daughter Marissa, her sister Lahti's children Tyler and Nadia, and Leann's children, Dana and Jason. Liza didn't want to go to trial; she just wanted to be sentenced. London and the rest of the family were glad to hear that. They didn't want to endure a trial after all they had been through. Liza was due to be sentenced in three months. London and the remaining family were going to be there. They were all upset about their father's death. London always heard men call Liza, "chocolate mama." Now she knew why. People seemed to be entranced by her beauty and controlled by her evil ways. Liza was extradited back to Paris and charged. London was prepared for that day. She wrote a statement just for her mother. The time had come to face her mother and for the grandchildren to face their grandma. The judge spoke, berating Liza relentlessly. Yet, Liza wasn't ashamed. She had the audacity to stand there with her head held high. London, with tears rolling down her face, said, "*I've thought about you tearing this family apart. As a mother, how can you murder your own children and grandchildren and not feel an ounce of guilt? You have robbed this entire family of peace, joy, happiness, and trust. You have taken my sisters, my bestfriends, and more. What happened? We were all so close. I thought you loved us and would never hurt us, yet look what you have done. The grandchildren that you spared have been robbed of their entire childhood and filled with nightmares. You've taken away their cousins, brothers, sisters, aunts, uncles, mothers, and fathers. These kids are in desperate need of therapy and will be for the rest of their lives because of what you have done. I don't recall anything such as this ever happening, several generations being wiped out by one person, by a woman at that. Your sentence should be severe. You may be my mother, but you are evil and wicked, and God will make sure you are punished his way. Because I am a Christian, I must forgive you, and I do. But these kids, they may or may not. I hope you know how to save your soul. If not, I feel for you because you have been totally consumed by evil. You can look at me calmly as I read this statement, and that shows you have no regrets for what you have done ... not one ounce of remorse is written on your face. Your daughters loved you, and you killed them intentionally, and without regret."*

Taking a seat, she wiped her tears away. Liza still wasn't fazed. The judge asked, "Is there anything you'd like to say before sentencing?" With a grin on her face, she spoke, "Yeah, London, I should have killed your bitch - ass first. I knew since birth you were going to be a problem, and as far as those kids standing there with you, fuck them! I was definitely going to knock them off, but the little snot - nosed brats grew up before I could. You're lucky the cops got to me. I made it to your door and was about to blow you away and have fun doing it. Your husband, Merck, he was my husband, too. In fact, all your sister's husbands were mine." The folks sitting in court gasped at her statement. The judge banged his gavel and yelled, "Life without parole. Now get this disgrace out of my courtroom!" Two weeks later, London filed suit against her mother in civil court. She won easily. She was awarded every penny of Liza's money and property. The kid's received money for the death of their father. London left open every store her mother and father owned. She opened one in Tennessee and ran it herself. London was glad she could start her life again. Estrada died in prison, after serving twenty - six years. She died from natural causes. London and her nieces and nephews kept the family business going. Thanks to London's hunches and the Holy Spirit, all of this came together and led to her mother's arrest. She was relieved to have justice for all. She could now move on. It would be rough, but she could do it because she had Jesus. Liza "Chocolate Mama" Hamgorium was cold busted by London.

CHAPTER NINE

Another Shocker

Twenty five years have passed. London had been getting an HIV test once a year for twenty-five years. Each test was negative. Even though her husband had it, she never contracted the disease. She was thankful to GOD for that. She knew she was supposed to have it, too, but GOD saw it differently. Liza was still in prison and very ill from HIV. Then, London received a call from the prison to let her know her mother had died.

London claimed her mom's body and had a proper burial for her. It was posted all over the news about her passing. Despite her horrible actions, people still admired her designs. A fan had her obituary printed.

In it, Liza's name read, "Liza (Chocolate Mama) Sadie Hamgorium." London thought nothing of it because that's who she was. This fan was a perennial fan; he had been to every fashion show. His name was Evan Ward. He was a photographer and a special guy. Walking up to London, he offered his condolences and asked if they could talk. London stepped outside to talk to Evan after the funeral. He told London that Leann was his daughter and that Berlin knew it. Evan said, "To keep shame off the Hamgorium name, your mom and dad paid me ten million dollars. Berlin adopted Leann, and it was never spoken of until now." Angry about what she was just told, she said, "If that is true, why are you just now coming around?" Evan interrupted, saying, "That's not all, Leann has a twin sister. Her name is Deanne, and she lives in California. Neither Liza nor Berlin wanted Deanne, and I was too young, so I put her up for adoption. She found me, but I never told her who her mother was. " In shock, London asked, "So you're telling me I have another sister out there?" Pausing, he said, "Yes. Would you like her number?" Skeptical at first, she agreed to take the number. Evan wrote the number down and asked, "Do you any other questions?"

"Yes, how did you know my mom and dad and when did you and my mom start seeing each other?"

"I was friends with your mom and dad. I wasn't as close to them like Connie and Dexter, but we associated in school. One day Liza and I went to the library to study and work a group assignment. She was my partner in class to do this project. We were working, talking, and laughing. The next thing I knew, your mom kissed me. We headed out to my car, and we had sex, in the back seat."

"How old were you both?"

"We were seventeen; it was a year before our senior year. Liza didn't know she was pregnant until it was too late for an abortion, so Berlin paid to keep it silent."

"Where would my dad get that kind of money at that age, Evan?"

"Your dad is a Hamgorium. He had a big trust fund. He paid me out of that."

"He paid you all this money and still had money left?"

"Like I said, he's a Hamgorium; he was rich before he was an adult."

Chapter Ten

The Meeting

Kicking back on her sun porch, London sipped on some tea. She stared into the sky. She thought about her niece, Dana. The poor girl had been through so much; she became a pill popper. She was just out there on the wild, but thank God she had no children. Thinking only good thoughts after that, London stared off into her vast land. She had sold the family business. It was worth 2.3 billion dollars. She bought herself a big mansion that sat on twenty acres. She bought each of her children and grandchildren a house. She paid cash. Her nephews and nieces received cash. They were set for life. London donated fifty million to the AIDS foundation and another fifty million to cancer foundations.

She decided to live her life and travel. She made reservations to go to Hawaii, Jamaica, the Bahamas, and the Virgin Islands. She didn't come home until she stayed two weeks in each place, and she had a ball. She decided that she would get with the sister she didn't know when she came back. She needed to clear her head and have some time to herself. London was enjoying her life. She knew this was living. She continued on her vacation adventure and thanked God for the blessings in her life. God gave her peace of mind and the finances to help others.

London returned from her trips refreshed. She got home, unpacked, and took a shower. It was 8:30 p.m. She thought her step sister would be home now. Slowly dialing her number, she cleared her throat as the phone rang. A sweet voice answered. Then London said, "Hello, may I speak to Deanne." There was a pause on the phone, then the voice asked, "May I ask who's calling, please?"

"My name is London. I'm her stepsister." The voice on the other end became angry, and said, "This is

Deanne, and I don't have any sisters, I am an only child ... " London quickly interrupted saying, "Your father's name is Evan Ward, and you found him, I assume, several years ago. You were adopted."

"Yes, that is true, but my dad never had any other children ... " London interrupted again saying, "He didn't tell you the whole story. I think you need to call and talk to him. You have caller I.D. You have my number. Please call me after you talk to him." Deanne hung up the phone and called her dad. He confirmed the story, and she was surprised by it all. She had no idea her biological mother was Liza Hamgorium.

Before calling London back, she had to gather herself. She was shocked her mom was famous. She was saddened, however, because she heard on the news about Liza's troubles and that she was deceased. Deanne called London back and apologized for her harshness. London understood and began to talk. They discovered they had a few things in common. They talked on the phone for hours. Before ending their conversation, they decided to choose a time to meet each other. London agreed to go to California to see Deanne. They were set to meet in three weeks. London had called and made reservations. Deanne was hurt. She felt she was cheated out of a good life. She began to think of ways to get some of that money, but then thought of it as evil. Deanne was a decent lady. London was on her way to meet her stepsister. Her rental car was booked, and she was ready. After arriving in California, she headed to a shopping mall to buy her step sister some gifts. She was nervous about meeting her. Upon arrival, she noticed her sister was living decently. Her house was modest and well kept. Her yard was well manicured and she was in a clean neighborhood. Stepping onto the porch, she rang the doorbell. When Deanne opened the door, London almost jumped out of her skin because she looked just like Liza. The eyes, skin, hair, and figure. With a smile on her face, Deanne told her to come in. London noticed her home was nice and neat inside. Taking London's coat, Deanne asked, "Would you like some tea?"

"Sure." Deanne led her to the kitchen where tea was sitting on the table. They sat down and began to talk. Deanne had a lot of questions, and London answered them. London had a long day. They decided that they would go out tomorrow. Driving to her hotel, she thought Deanne was a classy girl. She went to her hotel room and showered. She turned on the T.V. and got dressed to go down to the restaurant to eat. The restaurant was a seafood place, and London loved sea food.

The next day, London and Deanne went out to a movie, dinner, and shopping. London enjoyed having a sister again, and she thanked God for the blessing. London left for home after spending a week with her stepsister. When she got home, she called Marissa and told her about Deanne. Marissa was excited about having another aunt, after losing all of hers.

Deanne and London stayed in close contact. She came down to visit London two months after London visited her. When Deanne arrived, her jealousy revealed its ugly head again. London was living much larger than she was, but she kept her composure while there. Deanne thought Tennessee was a lovely place, and that London's place was beautiful, and she wished she had it. Before leaving, London gave Deanne an envelope and told her there was a check in it. She made her promise not to open it until she got home. Deanne smiled and was anxious to know the check amount. When she got home, she dropped her luggage on the floor and quickly opened the envelope. When she saw what it was, she screamed, "My God, a half million dollars." Deanne was beside herself. She immediately called London and expressed her sincere gratitude. She and London maintained contact throughout the year and they became closer than ever.

Chapter Eleven

Hope realized

The house two miles down from London was up for sale. She wondered who would buy it and be her neighbor. The vacant house didn't stay empty for very long, however.

Driving by one day, London noticed a man out in the fields working. Every day London saw that same man, so she figured he was the owner.

Later that year, a terrible storm rolled through Tennessee, and the power went out in London's neighborhood. She heard a knock at the door. When she opened it, she saw a man standing there in the rain. "My power went out. I figured yours went out, too. I just came by to check and see if you were ok. Oh, by the way, my name is David." London recognized him, shook his hand and invited him inside to dry off. She offered him some coffee, and they headed to the kitchen that was lit by several candles. London asked, "How do you like the house? You are the new owner, aren't you? I see you every day."

"I like it. It's roomy."

"David, if you don't mind me asking, what do you do?"

"I'm an artist, I own some art galleries."

"Oh, that's wonderful, I love art; it expresses the soul." With a smile on his face, he said, "That is exactly right." While enjoying each other's company, the lights came back on. He looked at his watch and noticed it was getting a bit late. He thanked London for the coffee and left.

As time went on, David and London developed a stronger friendship and spent a lot of time together. She enjoyed the time they spent at his art gallery and his home. London began to slack on her relationship with God because she was so consumed by David. Their relationship soon became intimate, and they fell in love. London was afraid of marriage because she had been widowed for so long, and her past experience was causing her to fear love. She knew it would eventually lead to marriage, but she wanted to enjoy their relationship for what it was now.

London began to shower David with gifts. She paid off his house and bought him a brand new car. She had more money than he could ever imagine.

Things were heating up more and more between them, and David was leaning toward marriage. They had been dating for a year now, and David felt it was time to ask. After he proposed, she said yes, but she just wanted to go to the Justice of the Peace to get married. She didn't want a big, fancy wedding. They set the date for the following month and decided that they would live together in David's home. Selling her home would allow them to have more money. London was ok with that because she was so in love with David.

Their marriage was a good one, and London was happy. She began working at her husband's art gallery and loved it. She knew that would happily occupy her time. The art gallery was doing well, and London decided to take art classes. She always wanted to; however, she was preoccupied with designing clothes and working for her parents when growing up. London was infatuated by David and knew she had found the love of her life. She was blessed beyond blessed. They attended church regularly and developed a stronger relationship with God. An annual family reunion was held at David and London's Tennessee home. London paid for the entire costs of transportation and accommodations for everyone. Correspondence with all parties was constant and gratifying. After all her tragedies, London finally found happiness that was lasting.